Secrets of Grady

GRADY LAKE MYSTERY SERIES
BOOK TWO

J.L. HYDE

Other Titles by J. L. Hyde:

Underground

Delta County

Summer of '99

Midnight in Delta County

Magnolia Court

Grady Lake

First paperback edition February 2024

Cover Design by Allsweet Studios and Brandon Kobs

ISBN 979-8-9871631-3-9 (Paperback)

www.jlhyde.com

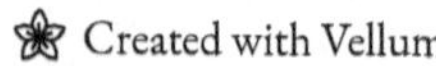 Created with Vellum

This book is for Christy, Katie, and Heather, who welcomed me home and made me feel like I never left. May the Toilet Paper Vixens ride again.

Grady Lake Character List

*Includes Spoilers from Book 1

- Katie Benard – Back home in Grady after a breakup. Sister of Malorie Rose. Works at the family resort.
- Malorie Rose – Missing for 20 years, discovered in an underground bunker on the property of family friend Richard Lowery
- Lou Benard – Aunt of Katie and Malorie, family matriarch, in charge of Benard's Lakeside Inn
- Dougie Benard – Malorie and Katie's cousin, works at the resort, briefly suspected in the disappearance of a tourist named Sammie Spencer, who was later found alive on the same property where Malorie was found.
- Brenda Benard – Dougie's mother, also lives in the lodge on the Benard property with the rest of the family.
- Deb Benard – Aunt of Dougie, Malorie, and Katie. Lives in the lodge.

- Charles "Chuck" David – Malorie and Katie's father
- Nicole Lowery – Best friend of Katie, Rich Lowery's daughter, operates the Grady Grab N Go.
- Richard Lowery – Nicole's father, arrested for the kidnapping of Malorie.
- Mae Lowery – Richard's mother, Nicole's grandmother, lives in an apartment above the Grab N Go.
- Lincoln Palmer – Millionaire owner of Palmer's Resort, arrested for kidnapping at the end of book 1.
- Fallon Palmer – Lincoln's wife, who dies at the end of book 1.
- Bradford and Benson Palmer – Lincoln's sons. Benson drowns under suspicious circumstances in book 1.
- Nolan Cowell – famous podcaster in town to cover the Malorie Benard case.
- Karli – Nolan's podcast partner
- Sheriff Nelson – first in charge of Grady's police force.

IT'S strange the things she couldn't remember. As the years went by, the sound of her mother's laugh went from a comforting track she played in her mind each night while attempting to fall asleep to a memory so distant she wasn't sure it was her mother's voice at all. She'd rock back and forth with her eyes closed, willing herself to conjure the answers to the most basic information from her upbringing. What kind of cereal did Katie eat in the morning? Who was Dougie's favorite NFL player? What kind of cigarettes did Aunt Lou smoke? Information that was once at the forefront of her young, innocent mind was gone. Poof. Vanished. Like her ordinary life never really happened.

A few years into her captivity—and who knows if it was two or four; she had no way of keeping track of time other than the changing seasons, which began morphing together during the years she wasn't allowed much sunlight—Malorie Rose did the unthinkable and snuck upstairs when she was as close to confident as possible that her captor was gone. She walked past the unlatched deadbolt in her underground room, tiptoed up the cement stairs, slowly worked the complicated locking mechanism on the hidden trap door above her (a series of clicks she'd heard several times a day for years, so she knew when it was locked or just simply closed), and peeked her head out to reveal the dusty wooden floor of Big Rich's cabin. By now, she was referring to him in her mind as *Rich, Rich the Son of a Bitch*, because, although he'd never physically hurt her, he was the reason she was in this predicament.

Malorie spent approximately two minutes above ground before her nerves got the best of her and she returned below, to her own personal hell. The most memorable thing about those two minutes? The sound of acorns. It was a windy fall day and Rich had most of the windows open in the cabin. Malorie had forgotten how violently the acorns were thrown from trees this time of year, often ricocheting off cars or pelting unsuspecting folks in the arm while they were out for an afternoon walk. For the first time in years, she smiled. The tiny thumps and cracks were like a song she used to love that lived in the back of her brain, waiting to be recalled. She may have even laughed out loud while remembering a forgotten story. It was late afternoon, and she and Katie went with their mom to Green Bay to shop for winter coats. They were returning to the car after a quick lunch at Old Country Buffet when their mother took a deep breath and looked to the sky to admire the beautiful fall day. At that very moment, a gust of wind shook the tree above them, and a single acorn came down, hitting Beth Benard directly in the forehead. At first, she was annoyed with the girls for laughing so hard at her expense, but their joy was contagious, and she soon erupted into a fit of laughter right along with them. She had a small, blue bruise between her eyebrows for days, and the girls giggled each time they passed her room and saw an open CoverGirl compact on the vanity, their mom leaning over in front of the mirror trying in vain to conceal it before her shift at the restaurant.

While underground, whether it was below Rich's cabin or the other handful of locations she had been kept over the years when Rich was convinced his home was going to be searched, her days became indistinguishable. There weren't many events that Malorie could remember clearly, even now that she was tucked safely in her childhood bed, surrounded by those who loved her most. One exception was the evening she had the greatest hope of being rescued. The night she was convinced her nightmare was over. The memory now was just as vivid as the moment it had happened. Just before bed, after another horrible day in captivity, she heard footsteps coming down the stairs that weren't like the others. They were lighter, they were hesitant, and when they arrived, Malorie realized they belonged to someone she had known her entire life. *Hallelujah, finally*, she'd thought, sucking in a quick breath of air, and rising to her feet.

But by the time she stood and opened her mouth to speak, she realized that familiar face had no intention of saving her at all.

Part One

One

I CAN'T SAY if it was ignorance, wishful thinking, or just plain naivety, but when I got lost in daydreams about having my sister back, it never occurred to me she wouldn't be the same sister I lost.

All I want is to lie under the covers with her, specifically the handmade quilt from Grandma Benard that's been folded at the foot of her bed since we were in elementary school, and stare at the ceiling while I fill her in on everything she's missed. I want to hold her hand while we run full speed and jump off the end of the dock into Grady Lake, kicking our feet off the soft sandy bottom to propel our bodies above the surface as high as we can. I want to hear about the boy she has a crush on in the next town over, the girl in her econ class who hurt her feelings the day before; I want her to beg me to take her Friday night shift at the restaurant so she can go to a bonfire with her friends. I want our lives back. I want Malorie back; the Malorie I knew.

As I sit on the edge of my bed and stare at the unmoving lump under the covers across from me, I can't help but think, *that's not my sister.*

She barely registered recognition when Dad and I entered her hospital room, which broke our hearts in pieces smaller than we thought imaginable. The doctor assured us it was because of the extreme dose of sedatives in her system, combined with eyesight issues and general confusion from being kept underground for twenty years. She was drugged, disoriented, and confused. It's been over forty-eight hours since she was released to come home, and we still don't have any answers. She has yet to talk to the detectives or counselors about the night she was taken or identify who was involved in her captivity all these years. No matter how high I turn the fan in our room, it isn't drowning out the sounds of the shutter clicks or questions shouted by journalists outside, which I'm sure isn't adding to her desire to speak.

"Mal," I say, barely above a whisper and possibly not loud enough to be heard over the fan or commotion outside. I walk a few steps closer to her, but she doesn't budge. "I'm going to make myself a Pop Tart; would you like one?" I haven't talked to my only sister in twenty years and all I can think to do is offer her a cheap, sugary breakfast pastry. Before I beat myself up too much over it, I accept that I need to cut myself a break; there isn't exactly a handbook for this type of situation.

When she still doesn't respond, I lean forward and tap her shoulder. I'm about to say her name again when it gets caught in my throat from the surprise of her jolting away from me the minute my index finger touches her. Wide-eyed, she flips over and pushes herself against the wall next to her bed. Both hands fly up in self-defense before relaxing slightly when she sees it's me.

"Mal, I'm so sorry. I'm so fucking sorry. I didn't think." I quickly spit the words out.

Her features soften. For the first time, I notice the fine lines etched around her eyes and scattered across her forehead. She's aged a lot more than the twenty years she's been gone.

"It's okay, Katie," she responds quietly. It's the first time I've heard her say my name since she's been back, and I nearly collapse from relief. Her voice, the one I've been playing in my mind every single day, is even sweeter than in the videos we watch every year on the anniversary of her disappearance. She now has the voice of a woman rather than an immature teenager, yet it's still so perfectly Malorie. I just want her to talk, talk, talk. I don't care what the subject is; I just want to hear her perfect voice a little more.

"How about that Pop Tart?" I ask with a smile. She shakes her head slowly and pulls the blankets over her head as she settles back into bed, turning away from me once more. I stifle a sob and remind myself that it's going to take a lot more time and patience before she's feeling like herself again. I can't take it personally. "If you change your mind, I'll be right outside," I tell her, trying my best not to let my voice quiver. She doesn't respond, so I slowly back out of the room, closing the door behind me.

When I walk down the short hallway and into the kitchen, I feel like a surgeon entering the hospital waiting room to announce news to a patient's family. Everyone is there and they are all silent and staring at me, leaning forward so they don't miss a word. All three of my aunts; my father; my cousin, Dougie; and my best friend, Nicole are all seated in various spots throughout the dining area, literally on the edges of their seats.

"Well, how is she? Tell us *something* for crying out loud," Dad demands after a few more seconds of silence.

I do my best to hold it together, but as I begin to say, "She's going to need more time," I lose it. I slap my hand over my mouth so Mal won't hear my sobs from our bedroom. I'm not much of a crier, but it's as if everything that has happened this week just came crashing down and the dam that was holding back my emotions finally breaks. Everyone in the room rushes to my side, wrapping me in their arms and whispering hushed words of comfort, also conscious of Malorie's presence a few doors down.

"Okay, okay, that's enough," I tell them after a few minutes of sympathy. "I'm just tired, that's all. I don't need a pity party."

"I knew you'd get back to being a little bitch," Nicole says, gently slapping me across the face before pulling me into a headlock and lightly tousling my hair. She's trying so hard to act like her world wasn't also turned upside down with the events of the last few days. Her father is currently in a holding cell, charged with kidnapping my sister, and humor is the only coping mechanism Nicole knows. Well, other than hard liquor, but Aunt Lou is making Nicole stay in my mom's old room so she can keep an eye on her alcohol consumption and general well-being. A firm believer in not using alcohol as a crutch, Lou always says, "We don't drink to feel better; we drink to feel *even* better. Only mix yourself a cocktail when life is good, or you'll start depending on a medicine that will never cure what ails you."

"Everyone, listen up," Lou begins. She is the oldest of the Benard sisters and her personality shows it. Although gruff and a little insensitive at times, Lou always takes charge and handles the toughest situations thrown at this family and trust me, we've had a lot. "We are going to give that sweet girl her space. She will talk when she's ready. She will eat when she's ready. She will come out of that room when she's ready. Until then, let's do our best to keep our heads above water. We've got to get the restaurant open tonight; we can't afford to be closed any longer. Nicole, do you have someone who can run the Grab N Go so you can stay in the kitchen with me?"

"Yes, ma'am, both of our new hires have keys, and they can handle an off-season afternoon," Nicole says to the only woman on this planet who scares her into saying ma'am.

"Perfect. Text them to get the place open, and I'll get you started on some prep work for tomorrow's lunch. Let's keep you away from the public eye for the rest of the week and far from nosy sons of bitches who ask too many questions," Lou tells her.

Nicole squints slightly before looking around the room at the rest of us. "Why would you do that for me, Lou? Don't you think you guys will be getting just as much unwanted attention?"

Lou grabs a prep apron off the counter along with her pack of cigarettes and responds, "Yeah, kid, but the difference is we've been dealing with it every day for twenty years."

Two

BEFORE ANYONE HEADS down to the restaurant to start prepping, we make a schedule that always places at least one family member in the lodge. Mal isn't showing any signs of wanting to talk, but we need a familiar face here when she's ready to come out of our bedroom. Benard's closes at 9:00 p.m. for the remainder of the off-season, so we should all be home for bedtime each night, which I hope is some sort of comfort for my sister. I just want her to feel safe, which is something I'm sure she hasn't felt in a very long time.

The first few days at the hospital were spent in the private family waiting room listening to Nicole apologize and plead for our forgiveness over and over again. We kept reassuring her that nobody is holding her accountable for the sins of her father, but it didn't seem to sink in until Lou leaned forward and slapped her hand on the oak end table next to Nicole. She looked her straight into Nicole's bloodshot eyes and said, "Everyone in this room has known you since the day you were born, and I speak for all of us when I say that you are family. You are not 'like' family or 'almost' family; you *are* family. We were all fooled by your father, not just you. If you're guilty, we all are. Do you understand me?" Nicole hung her head and nodded. That's the last time she's brought up the subject of her father. From that moment, she understood that we are in this together and we wouldn't dream of leaving her behind. Her Grandma Mae, Rich's mother, hasn't handled the news at all. She has locked herself in her small apartment above the Grab N Go and periodically responds to Nicole with a thumbs-up emoji after her repeated requests for Mae to at least confirm that she's alive and breathing.

The aunts are on the last day of the schedule when Dougie pipes in.

"I see you have me alone at the lodge with Mal on Sunday evening. I just want to make sure that's a good idea; I'm not sure how she feels about being alone around a man right now."

"Let me know if you see one," Nicole deadpans, slapping Doug on the shoulder before standing to leave.

We all smile. Every one of us. For the first time since we got home from the hospital, we have a reason to smile instead of spending every waking minute worrying about Mal's recovery or Rich's arrest or just how evil Lincoln Palmer might really be. Granted, each of us did a quick scan of the others to gain approval before our lips twitched, but alas, we all smiled.

"Alright, kids, quit dicking around and let's get prepped for a busy weekend. Katie Bug, you've got the first shift here. Do you need anything before we leave?" Lou asks me.

"Not a thing." I lie, knowing I could really go for a stiff drink, hot bath, and my sister's PTSD to be minimal. "I'll radio you if that changes," I add. Brenda grabbed one of the walkie-talkies from the restaurant to keep in the lodge, knowing that everyone working the restaurant shifts will be too busy to check their texts, and we need an immediate way to communicate any Mal-related issues.

After they all head downstairs, I lock and deadbolt the

door (at the aunts' insistence) and peek in our room to find that Mal hasn't moved. I get close enough to see her back rise and fall slightly with each breath and back out of the room, gently closing the door behind me. I grab a bag of chips, a can of Vernors, and sit on the oversized sectional in the family room for my first six-hour lodge shift. I think each of us has secret hopes of being the one waiting when Mal finally comes out of that room ready to talk. Until that moment, I'll be sitting here eating garbage and watching Netflix. Just as I grab the remote off the coffee table, my phone buzzes. It's a text from Nolan Cowell. He has kept a respectful distance since Mal's rescue; something I didn't think was possible for a true crime podcaster, but his hospital stay and road to recovery is most likely the reason.

"Asking as a friend, not a journalist: how are you?"

I sit with the question for a moment. Obviously, I'm not okay. But is Nolan really the person to pour my heart out to? Although he was with me for the most pivotal week of my life and is almost entirely responsible for figuring out Big Rich's involvement in Mal's disappearance, I've only known the man for weeks. The irony isn't lost on me that the pesky journalist who I couldn't get rid of quickly enough turned out to be the one to solve a twenty-year mystery and bring my sister home to me, suffering a bullet hole through his shoulder in the process.

"Hanging in there. How's Chicago and how is your shoulder?" I type.

Three little dots appear and stop several times before he replies.

"I'm still in Grady."

"The family and I gave you the exclusive on the story. You know we aren't going to change our minds, right? You don't need to stay here to convince us."

"I appreciate you guys so much. I'm working on the

episodes now; I just didn't want to leave until I knew you were okay."

Something stirs in me. I respond before I can reconsider.

"Want to have coffee tomorrow? I don't go in to work until noon."

Nolan takes an eternity to respond.

"I'd love to. Benard's?"

"Let's go somewhere a little quieter. Meet me at my car at nine?"

This time, he replies instantly.

"It's a date."

Less than two months have passed since I caught my fiancé cheating on me and moved back home, but it feels like two years with all that has happened. Getting involved with someone else has been the last thing on my mind, and although I've registered that Nolan is moderately good looking, reasonably charming, and extremely driven, I've never considered him a possible suitor. The little sister of Malorie Rose Benard and the podcaster who cracked the case? The entire country would lose their minds. I will admit, seeing my dad hug him when he took the elevator down from his hospital room to check on us did tug at my heartstrings. Dad held him in an awkward chokehold as he whispered *thank you, thank you, thank you* for a good minute and a half. Nolan, grimacing, was far too polite to tell Dad the embrace was too much for the man who was just shot days earlier. Luckily, the bullet missed anything major, and the doctors say he'll make a full recovery, hopefully with little to no effect on his range of motion.

I set my phone down and spend entirely too long scrolling through the streaming service's offerings before settling on a rom-com I've seen at least a dozen times. I kick my feet up on the couch next to me and reach for a handful of chips, only to find that they are beyond stale when I take my first bite.

Usually, I would let out a healthy sigh over the inconvenience of having to get off the couch once I'm comfortable to throw the chips away and find something else within its expiration date, but each time I consider complaining about *anything* this week, I'm reminded of what my sister has gone through during the last two decades. I don't have the right to complain about minor inconveniences anymore, and somehow, they all seem minor now that Malorie is home.

As I reach the pantry to search for my second-choice snack, I hear a slight rustling coming from our bedroom. I stop and close my eyes, convinced this will somehow aid in my hearing abilities.

She's moving. She's getting out of bed. Could she be coming out of the room? Does she know I'm here alone? No. I hear the door of our en-suite bathroom close. She's just using the toilet—the only thing she's done other than sleep since her return. When we first arrived at the lodge from the hospital, I watched her as we entered the back door and began to ascend the stairs. I expected her to look around wide-eyed, taking in all the sights she's missed for so long. Instead, Malorie just kept the blanket the hospital gave us for privacy wrapped around her shoulders and stared at the ground. Brenda, who arrived at the lodge before us to make sure Mal's bed was ready for her, held open the door with an optimistic smile, but Mal simply walked past her and directly into our room, shutting the door behind her. We were perplexed. We had all dreamed of a happy reunion with tears of joy and never-ending embraces, but instead we were delivered a zombie. A shell of the girl she was when she was taken. Of course, I'm not mad at her. I'm just furious at the situation. Even with all the events of the past week, I still don't feel like I have my sister back.

I freeze when I detect movement from the corner of my eye. It's the door to our room. It has cracked open. What do I do? Should I go see if she needs anything? Should I just give her space? I've grown into an insufferably independent adult and don't often yearn for my mother's guidance, but it sure would be nice right now. One of my first concerns when we arrived at the hospital was who would be the one to tell her that Mom had passed away while she was in captivity, but the doctor quickly informed us that she already knew. I don't know how the doctor obtained this information, but in our state of shock none of us thought to ask.

I decide to go check on her and I nod several times, a silly habit I picked up which somehow aids in reaffirming my choices. If I nod in approval, I'm telling myself it's okay. I've made the right decision. A few steps later, my hand is on the doorknob before my brain even registers that I've moved from the pantry. I slowly push the door open and flinch when it makes a high-pitched creak. Malorie is back in bed, but she's sitting up this time. Grandma's quilt is wrapped around her shoulders and she's staring at my empty bed. Her head gradually turns enough to make brief eye contact with me before darting back to the ground before her.

"Is it just you here?" she asks, barely loud enough for me to hear. She nervously licks her lips after speaking, like her mouth is no longer used to producing words. I wonder how much Rich and Lincoln conversed with her while those monsters kept her locked away.

"Yes," I say, and I barely recognize my own voice. I sound like I'm talking to a stranger, not my only sibling. "Everyone else went to work and they shouldn't be home until nine at the earliest."

"I think . . . . . . I think I might want something to eat," she says, once again meeting my gaze.

"Of course, Mal. Of course. What can I make you? I can have Dougie run us up a to-go order from the restaurant if you don't want anything around here. Whatever you're hungry for, I'll make it happen," I ramble, realizing mid-sentence how much I'm probably overwhelming her. "Did they . . . . . . did they at least give you hot meals?"

Her eyes grow wide. "*They*? You know?"

Did they honestly not tell her about the arrests when she was rescued?

"Yeah Mal, they arrested them both. Is that why you've been hiding in this room? Were you worried you were still in danger?" I ask.

"I guess a little bit. And I can't face Nicole. She has no family left . . . . . . all because of me."

"Whoa, it's not because of you. It's because of her psychopath father. You are a victim. And she has family left—she has Grandma Mae."

Mal scrunches her face and shakes her head slightly.

"No . . . . . . You said they arrested them both."

Three

I PLACE a hand on the door frame to steady myself. She must be confused. "Why would Mae be arrested?" I ask, not sure I'm ready for the answer.

"Oh, no. No . . . no," she says, shaking her head back and forth more rapidly with each word.

"Mal, was Mae involved in your disappearance? Your captivity? Both?" I ask. I am overwhelmed by my own frantic tone, so I surely am not doing anything to help my sister relax enough to tell me what happened. I need to chill and try this again. "I'm sorry, I didn't mean to freak out. You can tell me as much or as little as you want to. I didn't mean to be so aggressive."

Malorie hangs her head and appears defeated before speaking again. "I haven't seen her in a while. I honestly thought she might have died until I heard Rich talking to her about another girl who was missing."

"Sammie? Did they ever hold her down there with you? Or did they keep her with the others?" I ask, knowing I shouldn't. The counselor at the hospital warned us not to ask

Mal specific questions about her time away. She would tell us when she was ready. I couldn't help myself. My relationship with my sister has always been open and honest; we told each other every detail of our lives growing up and, in my mind, time isn't going to change that.

"The others?" she asks. She can't be serious. I search her eyes, and . . . she's telling the truth. She honestly doesn't know about the other girls. The ones that were found alive and the ones who weren't so lucky. Another set of remains were found on Rich's vacant property last week, bringing the total to nine girls who were kidnapped by Rich, Lincoln, and whoever else was involved in their fucked up little psychopath murder ring. Thank God Malorie was one of the lucky ones.

How is it possible she doesn't know about the other girls? Even if she wasn't held with them, Sammie and another girl were rescued from a bunker less than one hundred yards from where Malorie was found. The news has been repeating on every channel, every waking hour since their rescue. *Grady Michigan's Underground Bunkers of Horror.* I mentally replay Malorie's days since arriving at the hospital. They didn't turn on the TV in her room because they were concerned she'd be further traumatized and confused by the coverage. We left through the employee parking garage to avoid the reporters, drove home, and ushered her directly into the lodge, where she hasn't talked to us nor has she turned on a television. If she wasn't kept with these other girls, there's a real chance she has no idea she wasn't the only one. Lincoln Palmer is an asshole and a braggard; I cannot fathom that he kept my sister hostage for twenty years and didn't boast about his other conquests. I'm not sure what to say, as the doctor and detective both cautioned us about being the ones to break news to Malorie; they both agreed it would be better work for the trauma counselor who is on call for her when she's ready to talk.

"Mal, I'm not sure I should be the one to talk to you

about this. I don't want to be in trouble for saying things I shouldn't. Do you want to call the—" I begin before she cuts me off.

"Damn it Katie, what the hell do you mean *the others*? And who the hell else was arrested?" she asks through gritted teeth. I haven't heard her take this tone with me since the last time I borrowed her favorite sweatshirt without asking and dripped marinara sauce all over the front. I'd be lying if I said I wasn't still a little afraid of my older sister.

"Palmer, Mal. Lincoln Palmer. They didn't just take you . . . there were nine girls total. Three of you made it out alive. The detective is saying there might be more, but they have a lot of acreage to search. I'm so sorry; I assumed they kept you together. I'm so relieved you didn't have to witness them killing anyone; it's all that's been playing in my mind since we found out."

Mal stares at me with an intensity I don't think I've ever seen in her. She's searching my eyes for any hint that I'm not being honest, as if the subject of kidnapped and murdered girls is something I'd ever joke about. She's slowly shaking her head back and forth as her gaze falls from my face to the floor in front of her. She's shutting down again; I feel it. I made a huge mistake. Lou is going to kill me. I should not have even started this conversation with her, and now I can't take it back. I was just so excited that she was actually speaking, I didn't want it to stop.

"I'm not feeling very good. I think I'm going to lie back down for a while," she says, the momentary glimmer of life gone from her sleepy eyes as she retreats deep under the covers.

"But what about food, Mal? Aren't you hungry?" I ask.

"Maybe when I wake up," she mumbles.

I hold back tears and whisper to her before I leave the room.

"I love you, Malorie. I'm so glad you're home. I always dreamed you'd be back."

She doesn't answer or react. I bite the insides of my cheeks and hold my breath until I'm out of earshot. I walk hurriedly to the half bathroom at the other end of the living quarters and shut the door behind me, sit on the closed toilet, and wail into my shaking hands. This is nothing like I thought it would be, and I may have just made it even worse. I can't believe Mom isn't here for this. Dad is over at the restaurant, and I don't have the nerve to tell him what I've done.

After using half of the roll of toilet paper to dry the tears from my eyes and the rest of my face, I splash cold water and pat my cheeks until I see someone halfway resembling a human staring back at me in the mirror. If I could just get one good night of sleep, I know I'd be making more rational decisions. I'm just so tired. Last night was spent staring in the dark, across the room in Malorie's direction, imagining what she must be dreaming until daylight began to shine through the window between us. I can't keep this up or I'm going to go insane, but I also can't rest until I'm sure Malorie is going to be okay.

I tiptoe out to the kitchen and retrieve my phone from the counter next to the pantry. I saved the trauma counselor's number in my contacts; she told me to text or call her any time of day or night.

"Miss Temple, this is Katie Benard, Malorie's sister. I made a mistake and briefly talked about the arrests with her. She seems upset. I'm so sorry. Could you come tomorrow?" I type out.

Her response comes in less than a minute.

"Katie call me Dalia, please. Don't beat yourself up over it. She's been gone so long, it's natural to want to talk to her about all of it. Of course, I can come tomorrow—when would be a good time?"

I take a moment to consider the fact that I haven't run this by the aunts yet, but I'm sure they'd support the idea. I committed to having coffee with Nolan in the morning at nine, so eleven seems reasonable. That gives Dalia and Malorie an hour to talk before my shift begins at the restaurant. I'll feel much better being home during the session in case Mal needs me.

Dalia agrees to come to the lodge at eleven and I send a group text to the family letting them know about it. I don't consider it an emergency worthy of radio communication, especially because I can see the parking lot through the living room window and the restaurant is packed. I can only assume it's mostly lookie-loos and journalists, with annoyed locals simply wanting a stiff drink and a twice baked potato sprinkled amidst the chaos.

The quick response and plan set in place with Dalia calms my nerves enough to sit on the couch and press play on the old movie I'd selected, but I end up staring out the window above the TV because I'm mentally replaying every word during my exchange with Mal. I have so many questions but know that it's not in anyone's best interest if I ask them. I have to give her time. She'll talk when she's ready. We'll get answers when she's in the right headspace to give them to us.

Shortly after eight, I get a text from Dougie asking me to unlatch the deadbolt because he's on his way home from the restaurant.

"And Dad?" I ask.

"Nah, Lou has him cutting steaks and washing dishes, lol," he responds.

Lou has a quality I envy—the ability to make any man in her presence do things they would rather not be doing. It's fantastic. My eyes travel to the folded pile of sheets and blankets on the floor next to me. Dad hasn't gone back to his house in Marquette since we brought Mal home from the hospital. Since Nicole is sleeping in Mom's old room, Dad has been crashing on the couch. I don't have the heart to ask him how long he plans on staying, but despite the spotted history he has with the aunts due to his drinking and philandering, they seem to be content with the current arrangement.

A few minutes later, Dougie comes barreling in the main door to the living quarters, letting it swing open so swiftly it knocks into the entryway table. I spin around, putting my index finger to my mouth and shushing him so loudly, it probably has more chance of waking Mal than his entrance did.

"Are you nuts?" I hiss. "She's sleeping!"

"I'm not a fucking psychic, Katie!" he shout-whispers back.

I take a few steps closer to him and glance quickly down the hall in the direction of our bedroom where Mal is tucked in safely, hopefully in a deep rest. "Did you think she'd be out here playing Scrabble with me, dumbass? Sleep is all she's done since she got home."

Dougie drops his head and nods. "Will we ever really get her back, Katie Bug?"

"I think so," I lie. I cannot imagine the woman lying in Malorie's bed will ever be the same. "She just needs more time."

I usher him out on the balcony, which overlooks the restaurant. Although there's a chill in the air, the temperature is still mild for late fall in northern Michigan. I check behind us a few times through the patio doors, as if Mal is going to magically wake and sneak out to the living room to spy on our conversation. When I'm convinced we are alone, I scoot one of the Adirondack chairs closer to his and take a seat, motioning for him to do the same. We lean our heads close, and I replay my entire conversation with Mal while he listens, wide-eyed.

"Mae? Are you kidding me? And do you think Lincoln really had nothing to do with it, or is she protecting him?

Maybe it's like Stockholm Syndrome or whatever," he suggests.

I shake my head. "I don't know, Dougie. She seemed genuinely shocked that someone other than Rich and Mae would be arrested for this. I believed her when she said she had no idea there were other girls. But it's just not possible. How could she not know?"

"Lincoln has to have some sort of hold over her. Hopefully once she knows she's safe, she'll open up and admit it. One of the reporters who sat at the bar tonight told me that they are charging him with Benson's death. I'm telling you, that prick is a fucking monster," Dougie says, slowly shaking his head and glancing down in the direction of the kitchen door, which is on the backside of the restaurant. "Everyone will be getting home soon; have you decided how much you're going to tell them?"

"I'm going to respect Mal's wishes and hold off on telling anyone about Grandma Mae. Rich is in jail and Mae has locked herself up in her apartment; I don't see them being a threat to anyone at the moment. I think the news would push Nicole over the edge. Let's just see what happens with the therapist tomorrow and we'll go from there. I could see everyone in this family overreacting if I tell them everything that was said tonight."

"So this is a JDS," he says, raising his eyebrows a few times.

A "Just Dougie Secret" is a term he came up with when we were young. They were usually a result of me being annoyed with Nicole, Malorie, or both and having nobody else to vent to about them.

"Yeah, let's keep it a JDS for now," I respond with a sympathetic smile. "Another JDS for you—I'm having coffee with Nolan tomorrow."

He gives me a nod of approval.

"You could do much worse, Katie Bug. It's about time you found someone who actually deserves you."

"Oh, calm down. It's just a cup of coffee," I say, turning to go inside so he doesn't register the smile I'm attempting to hide.

Four

MY HEART HAS NOT ONCE FLUTTERED in Nolan's presence. I'd been so focused on Sammie's disappearance and defending my family's reputation on a nationally renowned podcast, the thought of him and me had never crossed my mind. Since Mal was found, *nothing* has been on my mind other than her. Today is the first time I'm seeing him since he was discharged from the hospital, and as he approaches my car—two minutes early, by the way—it's not only fluttering; my heart is doing backflips.

Any relationship I've ever had has been lust at first sight. I've thought about what they'd be like in bed within minutes of an introduction and normally got my answer within the first few nights. I often hear friends talk about how they were acquaintances with their husbands or wives first, sometimes for years, before feelings developed. I cannot fathom that scenario. You mean to tell me you just coexisted with a man, oftentimes while working forty-hour weeks alongside him, and not once felt an attraction until—BAM—one day you fell madly in love? Impossible. Well, until today. I wouldn't call it *madly in love*, but I'm definitely seeing Nolan in a different light, and now it occurs to me that I'm not sure he's even straight, let alone single. He's been so far off my radar we hadn't even had the conversation.

"Nice sling, my friend; did you get in a bar fight?" I greet him playfully and gesture toward his injured arm.

"It was the strangest thing; I creeped into the basement of a man I suspected to be a murderer, and would you believe it —when he found me, he shot me," he replies with a much more jovial vibe than I would have had I just taken a bullet through my shoulder trying to save a near-stranger.

I take a few steps in his direction and place my hand on his non-injured arm. "In case I haven't mentioned it today, I appreciate you very, very much. The whole family does. Whatever you need in life, we're here."

"Yesterday, I arrived at my cabin to find an expensive bottle of scotch from your dad, fresh baked muffins from Deb and Brenda, an array of freshly sliced deli meats from Lou, and a heartfelt text from Doug. I think your family is all caught up on showing their appreciation, I assure you."

I scrunch my face. "No gift from Nicole?"

"Nah, but she did flip me off last night when she took the trash out to the dumpster and then flung her still-lit cigarette butt at me, so I guess you could call that a gift."

"She's smoking again?" I blurt out. We've been spending so much time making sure she's not drowning herself in liquor, the thought never occurred to me that she'd pick up her other bad habits again.

"That's what you got out of that story?" He laughs and I shrug. "Okay, so where are we going for coffee, Miss Mysterious?"

I give him a quick wink. "Get in the car."

"Yes, ma'am," he replies, taking his time to navigate the door frame before settling in the passenger seat. I can't imagine how it feels to lose use of one of your arms, even if it *is* only temporary.

Nolan sniffs the air inside the car as he closes the door and reaches for his seatbelt. His eyes connect with the two fresh coffees sitting in the cupholders of my Highlander.

"Two splashes of oat milk, no sweetener," I say, motioning to his cup. "I just got them from the restaurant so we could go somewhere private and have a conversation without curious eyes on us."

"How did you know how I take my coffee?" he asks before lifting the lid to confirm that I did, in fact, nail the oat-milk-to-coffee ratio. He takes a sip and the edges of his mouth curve up into a slight grin.

"I had to listen to a few episodes of your damn podcast to make sure you weren't some hack-job wannabe journalist before I agreed to talk to you. You seem to yap about how you take your coffee at least once an episode. You trying to get a Folger's sponsorship or something?" I tease.

"Well, you must have liked what you heard if you agreed to let me interview you. And, for the record, I'm trying to get a Dunkin' Donuts sponsorship. C'mon."

"We better get out of here before Lou finds oat milk in the bar cooler. I plan to blame Dougie," I tell him while I shift my car into reverse.

I can see him smile and take another sip out of the corner of my eye as I pull out of Benard's Lakeside Inn. "Fucking yuppies," he mumbles in a decently accurate impression of Lou.

"So you *have* gotten to know Lou," I say with a laugh. *Fucking yuppies* is her response to any sort of request for food or drink that Benard's doesn't carry. She refuses to carry oat milk, veggie patties, gluten free buns, or egg substitutes and told me if I ever stock those items after she dies, her only mission in the afterlife will be to haunt me so intensely I shit my pants. That's a direct quote.

I take a left out of the gravel lot, and Nolan falls quiet as he watches the leaves slowly dropping all around us. A few acorns bounce off my car and I smile, remembering the time that my mother got hit by one right between the eyes. I don't remember where we were when it happened, but the three of us were together—myself, Malorie, and Mom. The only detail that isn't fuzzy is that Mal and I laughed so hard we cried and somehow laughed even harder when we realized it left a bruise. A sudden wave of sadness hits me when I remember, once again, that Mom didn't get to be here for Mal's homecoming. She died not knowing what happened to her oldest daughter and most likely assuming the worst. I keep daydreaming about what it would have been like for her to be in that waiting room with us, knowing Mal is alive and well and that we'd be able to see her in person before the night was over. The entire hospital stay still feels like some sort of strange dream to me.

About ten miles down the road, I turn onto a county road that will cut across to our destination. We haven't seen another car since we left the resort, and the kitschy signs at the ends of driveways that mark private family camps are growing scarce.

"Should I be worried?" Nolan asks, in a tone that assures me he isn't worried one bit.

"No, Mr. Cowell, you should be honored. I'm taking you to one of my favorite places on earth, and I assure you it's one you've never heard of."

"Color me intrigued," he responds, leaning forward to tuck his cell phone away in his leather messenger bag, which Nicole not-so-lovingly refers to as his *man purse.* He must not be concerned if he's putting away his only line of communication, not that he'd have cell phone signal this deep into the woods anyway.

"So, all jokes aside, how *are* you feeling?" I ask when we are less than a mile from the spot.

"Oh, they have me on enough medicine to calm the pain when it gets too bad. From what I've researched, it seems like one of the best places to be shot, if there is such a thing."

"Of course, you've been researching your injury instead of just resting," I tease.

"Hey, I do a lot of typing and editing. I had to make sure having my full range of motion back is a possibility."

"Well, is it?" I ask.

"Barring any major setbacks, I think I'm going to be just fine, KB."

I'm startled to hear my nickname on his lips. He clocks my reaction and quickly interjects.

"Sorry, I've just been editing the interviews with Dougie and Nicole, and I think I've probably heard them call you KB about a million times. It just slipped out."

I steal a glance to see his cheeks are slightly reddened.

"You brought my sister home. I think you've earned the right to call me KB," I respond with a smile, which causes the immediate release of his hunched shoulders.

"I didn't bring her home; I just caught the bastard in a lie and investigated," he says.

"That bullet hole in your shoulder begs to differ," I counter.

I reduce my speed and pull into a clearing in the woods to our left and shift the car into park when we have a full view of the small, uninhabited lake.

"To be fair, I've seen more than a few eighties horror movies that begin this way, so if you want to take this moment to explain why we're here, that would be much appreciated," Nolan says, setting his coffee back into the cup holder between us.

"This lake that you're looking at is one of my favorite places in the whole world," I tell him.

"Well, what's it called?" he asks.

I smile.

"John's Lake."

"I sense a charming small-town story behind that name," he says. I know he loves all the Northwoods stories he's heard since arriving in Grady, and it saddens me that, until last week, most of them had come from Big Rich. He was a great storyteller.

"Well, a guy named John bought forty acres back in 1982 and didn't realize there was a lake in the middle of the acreage. He owned Beaver Trapping Supply Store and—"

"Wait," he interrupts. "There is an entire store just for beaver trapping supplies and they sell enough to stay in business?"

"Oh, his last name was Beaver. They sold all sorts of animal trapping supplies and, yes, they did more business than they could handle around here. Once Mal disappeared and Grady Lake became tourist central for the morbidly curious, he started letting us locals come here to get away from the noise."

"Well, that's so nice of him. And he still doesn't mind that you come back here?" Nolan asks.

I turn in my seat to face him. This is my favorite part of the story.

"John Beaver died in 2018 and donated the acreage to the city of Grady. His only stipulation is that it remain a hidden gem for the locals and that the walking path surrounding the lake be named after Malorie. We've kept both promises."

He scans the lake with a fresh perspective and smiles contently.

"I can see why it's your favorite place," he says.

"If I'm being honest, it's not so much to do with him

naming the path after my sister. It's because every winter at the end of January, swans migrate here. You can park right here in the middle of the freshly fallen snow and watch the swans for hours. It's magic. The best part is, we've all kept it a secret. There aren't any pictures online, and there's no way that a tourist could find out about it unless a local shows them."

"I'm a little hung up on this swan migration story. Where are they the rest of the year? Why do they specifically choose this lake? What do they eat?"

"Nolan, I'm not a damn zoologist. I have no idea. All I know is that it's the most beautiful thing I've ever seen, it happens every year, and I'm telling you this because I want you to know I trust you and you can trust me."

Nolan registers the fact that I didn't just bring him here for peace and quiet; I brought him here because it's important to me and I need to trust and have a very real conversation with him about Malorie.

"Look, I haven't known you nearly long enough to be telling you the most personal bits of information dancing around my sleep-deprived brain, but I need someone to talk to. Malorie finally spoke to me for a minute last night and the little that she did say didn't make any damn sense."

"Of course you can trust me, Katie. What did she say?"

"I need this to be off the record," I tell him and lock my eyes with his to show him how serious I am. "I haven't even talked to the aunts or my dad about it yet."

"You got it," he agrees, although I'm sure it was reluctant. This is the story that is going to change his career forever, and he's alone with the sister of the victim without being able to use anything I say for the podcast.

"She told me she never saw any other girls and she seemed very surprised that Lincoln Palmer was also arrested," I tell him, leaving out the part about Mae's involvement because, frankly, I'm just not ready to have that conversation with someone other than Dougie.

Nolan doesn't seem to be as shocked as I expected him to be by this news.

"Well, that kind of makes sense, considering some information that I was given by an anonymous source at the hospital who overheard Sammie being questioned."

"What do you mean?" I ask, not wanting to wait another second to hear what he has to say.

"According to the source, when given a photo lineup to identify her second captor, Sammie clammed up for a while and finally said none of them resembled the person who took her out of the woods. When shown Rich's picture specifically, she said she'd never seen that man before in her life. Her mom told the investigators that Sammie needed rest and refused any further questioning for the rest of the night."

Five

WE STAY by the lake for an hour and talk, mostly about Mal. I confess my feelings about how strange it is to have her home when nothing about her feels like family. He reminds me to have patience and asks me to envision how happy our lives are going to be a year from now when Malorie has settled back into her old life and the news media's attention has long since shifted to the next scandal. He's right, and that vision might just get me through this.

When we pull back into Benard's, I see Dalia getting out of her silver sedan parked next to the back entrance of the lodge.

"That's Mal's therapist. I hate to cut you short, but I want to go greet her before she goes in," I quickly say to Nolan before putting my SUV in park. His eyes follow Dalia as she opens the back door of her car and reaches in to retrieve a shoulder bag.

"Their first session?" he asks without breaking his gaze.

"Yes, but that's all you're getting out of me. You damn journalists are ruthless."

"But we're friends . . . you took me to John's Lake," he says while comically batting his eyelashes at me.

"Yeah, yeah. Okay, I'm working from noon until eight at the restaurant; stop in if you want to chat more."

"You got it," he responds with a wink so subtle I nearly miss it. He grabs his bag, takes his empty coffee cup *and* mine (swoon), and waves goodbye as he walks across the property toward his cabin. It's directly across from the one Sammie and her family were staying in, but they checked out when she was discharged from the hospital yesterday and sent a family member to collect their belongings and bring their keys back to the front desk at the lodge. The woman, who identified herself as Sammie's aunt, also left two thousand dollars in cash to cover their stay and meals because Lou refused to give them a bill. With everything going on, we've been closed more often than not and even when we're open, rising supply costs have made margins the tightest they've ever been. Lou wanted to do the right thing and house a distraught family while they searched for their missing daughter, but I'm certain she is relieved to have the money to help with payroll this month.

"Dalia?" I speak just loud enough to get her attention before she opens the back door. "Nice to see you again. It's Katie, in case you forgot."

When she spins around to face me, her smile is so warm it makes me wonder if it's something they teach in school for treating trauma victims.

"Katie Benard! Of course I remember you. I'm not sure I've ever seen such a beautiful fall day. We are so lucky to live in this state, aren't we?"

I've only felt this way about a handful of people in my life, but Delia feels like sunshine. She feels like Christmas morning, like watching your favorite show. If she has anywhere near this effect on Malorie, she might just get her to open up after all.

"We sure are," I answer with a quick smile. She takes a few

steps back in my direction and places her hand on my left shoulder.

"I cannot imagine what you and your family are going through right now. Hell, what you've been going through for twenty years. I promise you I'm going to do everything in my power to make your sister feel comfortable enough to open up so we can begin her healing process. I will do my best to make this transition as easy for you and your family as possible, but I need to ask for your patience. Her amount of time in captivity is something we've seen less than a handful of times in history and it's as close to uncharted territory as we have in this profession. It's going to be a lot of trial and error, but I promise you we are going to get your sister back. She will know she's loved and safe."

Fantastic, I'm crying again.

"I'm sorry, I'm just so tired," I say, still not sure why I feel the need to apologize for my emotions.

"Katie, you have nothing to apologize for. Also, I don't mean to overstep my boundaries, but I wanted to remind you that the victims' fund has more than enough resources to afford some sessions for yourself or any member of your family who may want to talk. I'm fully dedicated to the Benard family for the foreseeable future."

I wipe my eyes. "Buckle up, Dalia, *you* might be the one needing therapy when you're done with us."

She wholeheartedly laughs at my joke. I'm talking head thrown back, hand over her heart, absolutely tickled by my humor. I adore this woman. I'm confident Malorie will, too.

"Ready?" she asks, opening the door for me.

"Ready as I'll ever be," I respond, forcing a smile.

I climb the stairs a few steps in front of Dalia and fish around in my purse for the keys to the family's living quarters. Before this week, we hadn't locked the door in so long that we had a hard time even locating a single key between us so we could make copies. The aunts aren't worried about the reporters; it's the unstable, true-crime-obsessed out-of-towners who may get a little too curious when they find out our home is so close to the restaurant and cabins.

When I open the door, I'm relieved to see that everyone appears to be gone to work except Lou. She has the "Malorie Shift" here at the lodge this morning, which I know she's happy to do, but her manic pacing in the hallway says that she'd rather be managing the restaurant operations and doesn't exactly trust the others to handle it without her.

"Anything?" I ask as Dalia and I enter the living quarters, knowing there's very little chance Mal has come out of the room this morning.

Lou shakes her head and gives an apologetic shrug. "She did eat the oatmeal I set on the nightstand next to her bed this morning. When I came back in from having a smoke, the empty bowl was set outside in the hall. That's progress."

Well, I suppose the constant concern over Mal starving to death is one less worry I'll have today.

Lou greets Dalia and they briefly speak in hushed tones about the plan for this morning and what to expect. I ask her if she'd like me to go into the bedroom and let Mal know that she's here and why.

"No need. She and I met at the hospital, and I'm confident I can handle the interaction today. If you two wouldn't mind waiting out here, I'm going to go reintroduce myself and see if she's capable of having a session today."

"Would you . . . like anything to eat? Drink?" I ask.

Dalia gives me that warm smile again and politely declines. She opens her bag, which is now sitting on our kitchen island, and retrieves a notebook and pen. "I'll peek my head out if I need any assistance," she tells us before she turns to walk down the hall toward my childhood bedroom, her dark curls bouncing with every step.

Lou and I both pull up a chair at the kitchen table and collapse into them as Dalia knocks twice, enters the room, and shuts the door behind her. Lou looks as tired as I feel. I've been so consumed with being the sister of Malorie Rose Benard this week, I've completely neglected to consider what the rest of the family is going through. Lou, who has become the unlikely matriarch of this family since the passing of my mother and grandparents, is having to navigate the complicated issues surrounding Malorie's return, operate a restaurant so we can all keep a roof over our heads, deal with one of her closest friends being arrested for her niece's kidnapping, and she's doing this all without her own beloved sister—my mother.

"How are you holding up?" I ask, and the words sound foreign coming out of my mouth. Nobody checks up on Lou. Lou is the stable, predictable, stoic one in charge.

Her awkward smile is her acknowledgement of how odd it is for anyone to be asking about her well-being, specifically me.

"I'm a tough broad," she begins, before tapping one of her calloused hands over mine. "But so are you."

"I feel like this last week has been a dream. I still don't believe she's home," I say.

"I know having Mal home is nothing like you dreamed it would be, kid. I understand that. But, like Dalia says, we have to have patience. We have no idea what that sweet girl has been through the last twenty years, specifically at the hands of a man she's known her whole life and a rich asshole she knew well enough."

Guilt shoots through me, remembering that I haven't disclosed what I've learned about Lincoln Palmer's possible non-involvement in the situation. I'm still working through my thoughts on the matter, and I don't want to tell Lou anything until I'm sure. Once the police have a more productive interview with Sammie and the seventeen-year-old survivor who was found unconscious in the bunker, we should have some more definite answers about who was involved. The idea that Rich kidnapped Malorie while Lincoln simultaneously kidnapped and murdered girls on the same property is simply impossible. Also, Sammie's mom, Brandi, told me at the hospital that she said *two* men were holding her captive. Until I spoke with Nolan this morning, I assumed those two men were Lincoln and Rich. At this point, it's all questions and very few answers.

My phone begins to vibrate in my purse, which is hanging on the hook next to the door. The constant buzz denotes a call rather than a text, which is so rare my heart momentarily stops. My generation has collectively morphed into only-for-emergency calls, surviving solely on texts to communicate. Even Lou's face is screwed up in curious wonder. I jump to my feet to retrieve it and stop in my tracks when I flip the screen over to see *Asshole* flashing across the screen. It's the name I changed my ex-fiancé to in my contacts after I caught him cheating with the girl who sold us morning bagels at the shop down the street. Somehow, the worst part of it all was losing the freshly baked poppyseed bagel topped with garlic and herb cream cheese from my morning routine.

"It's Dave," I announce.

"That son of a bitch. Let me answer it; I need someone to let my frustration out on anyway," Lou grumbles.

I give a slight grin and shake my head before answering the call right before it goes to voicemail.

"This is Katie," I answer in my most professional tone. I don't want him to think I even have his contact saved anymore. He laughs in response, which nearly sends me into a rage, but I control my emotions.

"Did you really delete my number, Kate?" he asks. He is the only person in life who has ever called me Kate. It's either Katie, Katie Bug, or KB. I am not a Kate.

"How can I help you, Dave?" I ask, still in my customer service voice.

"Well, I heard the news and wanted to give you a few days before I called to check in on you."

"How considerate of you. I'm doing just fine, thank you."

He dramatically inhales and exhales, which used to stress me out, frantically guessing at what I did to annoy him, and now I could not possibly care less. What a feeling.

"Christ, I'm just trying to have a conversation with you and show that I care. Can we not be adults here and have some sort of friendship?"

"Oh, to show you care? Is that what you were doing after I worked seventy hours a week supporting you during grad school so you could get an entry level job in a lab and fuck the bagel girl from down the street? You don't get to be my friend, Dave. Friends don't intentionally hurt each other."

My heart rate is rapidly increasing, which disappoints me that I'm letting him have this effect on my body.

"Well, I'm sure you'll be happy to know that *bagel girl* and I are no longer together, and I can't stop thinking about how betraying you was the worst mistake of my life," he says, and his tone infuriates me. It's the one he uses when he's lying to his mother about why he didn't return her call or the reason he's not coming home for Christmas.

"I haven't slept in a week so I'm sorry to say the cleverest response I can come up with at the moment is *get fucked*," I spit out before jamming my thumb on the large red button to end the call.

Lou stands and claps as I walk back to the dining room and toss my phone on the table. As soon as it lands, the backscreen is once again lit up with Dave calling. I reach for it, but Lou retrieves the phone first and immediately answers the call. His unbearable voice comes booming through the speaker so loudly, I can hear it from five feet away.

"Did you just hang up on me?"

"I don't know, asshole, did it sound like this?" Lou exclaims before ending the call.

"Block his number, kid," she says, handing the phone back to me. A few clicks later and it's done.

I grab us both a ginger ale from the fridge and we spend the next thirty minutes talking about my life in Lansing and the specifics of my breakup with Dave. Although Lou is aware that Dave cheated, she's never asked for details, and I've been too exhausted to discuss them. Today, however, it's a perfect way to pass the time and officially close the chapter on my relationship with him instead of sitting here in silence and wondering what, if anything, Dalia and Malorie are discussing.

An hour after their session began, Dalia gently emerges from the room I share with Mal and closes the door behind her. I'm not sure if the smile she's wearing signifies that she's trying to soften the blow of bad news she's about to deliver or that she's pleased with Malorie's progress today. Lou and I sit in silent anticipation as she walks to the table, which seems to be happening in slow motion.

"Well, ladies, it was a rough start, but we had a turning point about thirty minutes into our session," she tells us.

"What happened?" Lou asks.

Dalia looks at me before responding.

"She heard Katie on the phone with who I presume to be an ex-boyfriend. She fell quiet and listened to you both for a moment . . . and then she laughed."

Six

I'M on cloud nine as I clock in for my shift. *She laughed.* Malorie laughed! My unhinged response to my narcissistic ex-fiancé made her laugh. There is hope. There is real hope that my sister can slowly emerge from that cocoon and regain her old qualities, the ones that made her so very Malorie. I am on top of the world.

"You're late," Dougie says as I clock in at 12:04, barely looking up from the lime he's currently slicing into wedges.

Deb and Brenda are in the kitchen, filling drinks for customers of the early lunch rush. They both steal glances at me to make sure I appear okay, both knowing I've never been late for a shift in my life. I tie my server apron around my waist and clap my hands together before declaring, "She laughed."

"What?" Brenda asks, surely thinking she misunderstood me.

"Dalia just finished their session. She wasn't speaking much, but she overheard me yelling at Dave on the phone and Dalia says she laughed. Can you believe it?"

I knew the family would be relieved at this revelation, but I didn't expect such an extreme response. Deb, Brenda, *and*

Dougie all stop what they are doing and run toward me with open arms. The three of them hug me so tightly, I can barely breathe.

"She really laughed? Is Dalia sure?" Deb asks, tears forming at the corners of her eyes.

"Was it like a big Malorie laugh or just a smile and a chuckle? Did you hear her laugh?" Dougie asks and his eyes are also glistening.

Before I can answer, Dad peeks his head out of the prep room and yells, "What are you guys going on about?"

"Mal laughed!" Brenda exclaims.

Dad drops a Cambro container, which scatters iceberg lettuce all over the kitchen floor and runs over to hug me, pushing the rest of the family out of the way.

"What did it sound like? What made her laugh? Did she come out of the room?"

"Guys, guys, calm down," I say, but I'm smiling so big that I can barely finish my sentence. "Dalia can't tell me exactly what was said because of patient doctor blah blah blah, but she said that Mal overheard me going off on Dave when he called, and she laughed. She fucking laughed!"

"She's going to be okay. I just know it. My little girl is going to be okay," Dad says and there's not a dry eye in the room.

"Okay, I saw how full the lot is. We need to focus. Let's get through this shift and then we'll talk about it some more," I say. "What section do you have me in?"

"Section one," Dougie answers, before adding, "If we call Dalia, do you think she could recreate the laugh for us?"

Nobody answers him, but we all smile while I grab my order pad and the rest of the family returns to whatever restaurant duties they were in the middle of before I interrupted their tasks with my ridiculously good news. How am I going to get through this shift when all I can think about is getting back to the lodge to check on Malorie? What if she's up there in the family room with Lou now, laughing up a storm? I don't want to miss a minute of it, but I know we need to get these customers served.

The next few hours are a blur of club sandwiches, draft beer, and a million questions about how it feels to have my sister home, mostly from people I've never met because locals know better. The ones who have known me my entire life simply pat my shoulder and tell me they are so happy to hear the news that Mal has come home and to call them if there's anything we need. One of my very favorite locals, Curtis Rivers, sits in my section with his five-year-old son, Brogan, about halfway through my shift. He is especially my favorite on days like today because Curtis shows no emotion, ever. I attended his and his lovely wife Lynn's lakeside wedding a few years back, and according to his face, you'd think we were attending a funeral. During his speech at the reception, he said it was the single happiest day of his life and that Lynn was the only thing in this world that made him happier than a day of fishing. He didn't smile, but I will admit, he looked reasonably content as they entered the back of a rented limousine, hand in hand, to be whisked away to the airport for their honeymoon. Despite spending most of the week deep sea fishing, Lynn reported that they had a splendid time in Florida.

"Your sister back?" he grunts as I set down his perch dinner and a grilled cheese for Brogan.

"Now where in the world did you hear that?" I tease.

"It's on every news channel in the nation," he deadpans.

"Yes, Curtis, I was only joking. Mal is home safe, and we are all very thankful for that," I say with a smile.

"What do you hear about the bluegill this week?" he asks. My sister's homecoming after twenty years may be more important than the fishing conditions, but just barely.

"Yeah . . . I haven't really been talking to too many fishermen about their catches this week, on account of the fact that my sister was rescued from an underground bunker where she was kept for twenty years," I return his deadpan.

"Alright, well if you hear of anyone having luck by the north cove, shoot me a text."

I have never met a more oblivious man, yet it's somehow refreshing to encounter someone so uninterested in the details of my family's life.

"I'll be sure to do that, Curtis," I tell him before turning to check on my other tables.

When they are nearly finished with their meals, I drop the check off face down on the table.

"I'm going to catch the biggest fish in Grady Lake, and Dad is going to mount it over the fireplace," Brogan tells me as I wait for Curtis to retrieve a few bills out of his wallet and hand me his normal fifteen-percent tip. Not high enough to be considered a big tipper, not low enough to be insulting.

"Is that right? Well, be sure to have your dad bring you in here to tell me about it once you have him caught. I'll make you a special milkshake to celebrate," I tell him, bending down to ruffle the blonde shaggy hair on his head.

"Did you hear that, Dad? Miss Katie says I can have a milkshake," Brogan boasts, his tiny body bouncing up and down on the booth.

"We probably need to remind Miss Katie that little boys your age never forget a damn thing so she better make good on that milkshake once we catch our monster fish," Curtis says in his usual dry tone.

"Miss Katie will be happy to make you both milkshakes," I say, smiling at the adorable young boy.

"Milkshakes mess with my stomach," Curtis tells me.

"I know," I answer with a wink, taking the payment and check from his hand and turning on my heels to walk back to the kitchen.

The mood in the back of the restaurant is that of pure joy. By now, the handful of non-related employees who stay on through the off-season have heard the news about Malorie and are equally as elated. Although our prep cook, Paul, knew Mal before she was taken, the other two off-season employees were too young so they only know what they've seen on the news. Paul went to high school with us and took a job in the kitchen at Benard's to help support his mother after their father took off in the middle of the night with no note or forwarding address. Over twenty years later, he says he has no desire to work anywhere else. He gets paid a fair wage, only works the morning shift, and is home every night to make dinner for his mother. I often find myself wanting more for Paul before remembering that this may not be what I'd want for the rest of my life, but it seems to be what makes him happy, so who am I to judge?

As I take a two-minute breather from waiting on the guests in my section, it hits me that Nicole isn't here. She's at the Grab N Go this morning because both of her off-season employees needed the morning off. I cannot wait to tell her about Mal. It will be just the dose of good news she needs to help get her out of her funk. I can't imagine what it's like to learn your father is a complete monster, but I know my family will continue to do whatever we can to make sure Nicole knows she's one of us.

The rest of the shift goes as smoothly as it can with the amount of business we are seeing as a result of the news. Thankfully, several tables seem oblivious to the fact that I'm Malorie's sister. I hear them discussing the events as I deliver food and drink refills, and they barely register my presence. An hour before I'm due to go home, Nolan walks through the door, and once again my heart starts pounding so rapidly, I'm convinced he can see it beating through my work uniform. The host grabs a menu and looks around the room for an open table as I rush to the front and retrieve the menu from her hand, politely telling her that I'll seat this guest. I blush when she recognizes what I'm doing and smiles at us both.

"How was your day?" Nolan asks, and it just feels good to be asked by someone I'm convinced genuinely wants to know how I'm doing. I lead him to the same table I always seem to seat him at, next to the window overlooking the lake.

"Well, I've got big news," I tell him, pulling up a chair because I only have one other customer currently in my section and he's elbow deep in the spaghetti special.

"Well, spill it," he says with wide-eyed anticipation.

"When the therapist got done with her session, she let Lou and I know that there was a turning point halfway through when Mal *laughed*. I'm talking an actual laugh. Can you believe it?"

"Oh my god, Katie. That gives me chills! Did she say what made her laugh?"

My cheeks slightly redden once more.

"Remember I told you I moved home after my fiancé and I broke up? I'm not sure if I mentioned this detail, but it's because he cheated. Well, I hadn't talked to him since it happened . . . until today when he called and I gave him an earful. Apparently, Mal overheard my end of the conversation and she actually laughed."

"What kind of idiot cheats on Katie Benard?"

"I know, right?" I say with a smile. "So, what are we drinking tonight?"

"I'm sticking to Coke, unfortunately. My shoulder has been throbbing, so I took some pain meds and apparently, they don't mix very well with alcohol."

"How responsible of you, Mr. Cowell. I'll be right back with your ice-cold Coke."

I'm involuntarily smiling as I fill the glass with ice and

stick it under the soda fountain in the kitchen. It's been a while since I've had so much to be excited about.

"Oh, you've got it bad for your new little boyfriend," Dougie says, and I realize he's been standing at the end of the expo station staring at me since I entered the kitchen.

"Shut the fuck up, Dougie."

I hear gravel fly outside the restaurant and peer out the small kitchen window to see Nicole's Jeep pulling in. I crouch down by the back door to scare her when she enters but regret the decision as I jump out and notice her eyes are red and swollen.

"Oh my gosh Nic, what happened? What's wrong?"

Dougie hears me and runs over, both of us at Nicole's side awaiting her response. She hangs her head and wipes her nose on the sleeve of her flannel before raising her gaze to meet mine.

"I went upstairs to see Mae after my shift and she wouldn't answer the door. I finally told her I was using the spare key to get in, and when I did . . . she was in bed. I thought she was just taking a late nap, but when I touched her hand, she was cold. She's dead, KB. Grandma Mae is dead."

Seven

DEFEATED. Exhausted. Discouraged. I think we're all experiencing the same emotions as we watch Mae's casket being lowered into the ground at the cemetery where we buried Benson Palmer just weeks ago.

Nicole has barely said a word all day. Despite her full understanding of the many reasons Big Rich wasn't allowed out of jail for his mother's funeral, it still enraged a grieving and nonsensical Nicole. Malorie, understandably, has once again fallen silent. The only words she has said all week were when she whispered her request that I not tell anyone else about Mae's involvement in her captivity. After all these years, I still can't lie to my sister, so I came clean about telling Dougie but she didn't seem upset by it at all. Dougie has always been the keeper of our secrets. He and I have both kept our word to not tell anyone else what we know. Is there any point now, anyway? She's gone. It's Malorie's secret to keep. She can tell Nicole if and when she feels ready.

It's a conflicting range of emotions saying goodbye to the woman who has been like a mother to me for as long as I can remember, knowing she had something to do with Malorie being held in her son's basement. How in the world has she been able to look me in the eyes for the past twenty years? She's laughed with me, cried with me when Mom died, and welcomed me home with open arms after my breakup with Dave. Despite her evils, I find solace in the fact that she seemingly died in her sleep. She has told Nicole and me on more than one occasion that it's how she hoped to go. "Lucky bastard" was her response each time word traveled back to her that an old acquaintance had died of natural causes.

Everyone is understandably curious when the Benard family shows up to the funeral of Richard Lowery's mother. Rich kept our sweet Malorie underground for two decades against her will, and now we are here to mourn his mother. What a tragic, twisted web of secrets this small town has become. It's no great surprise when outsiders don't grasp the dynamic between families who have known each other for generations. Brenda had a few sips of mulled wine the other night and let it slip that Aunt Lou and Rich were once seventh-grade sweethearts. Could you imagine the shitstorm if a photo surfaced of them together at that age? It would be the top headline for a week: *Aunt of Malorie Rose Benard Once Dated Her Captor.*

Lou closed the restaurant for two hours to allow Mae's family and friends to gather and enjoy a warm meal after her service. Malorie, of course, is holed up in our room and refused my offer to bring her a plate. I did, however, catch her gazing out the window when I stepped out back to find Nicole and Lou smoking cigarettes behind the restaurant, staring at the gravel and not saying a word. I didn't call any attention to it because I didn't want to scare her enough to return to the bed with covers thrown over her head. Standing at the window is a solid improvement from where she's been.

Once the mourners disperse and the aunts prepare the restaurant to reopen to the public, Lou tells me to take the night off to spend with Nicole. I don't argue; I could really use a night off my feet that isn't spent lurking outside our bedroom door, praying Mal will come out and ask me for a sandwich. I check in with Olivia, a sweet girl we recently hired to run the front desk in the lodge, and she tells me that cabin five is unoccupied tonight, so I get the keys from her and tell her to call me if we have any last-minute requests for it, which I'm certain we won't. Even with the added traffic in Grady, lakeside cabins aren't exactly a late-night, last-minute decision. Most of our reservations are made weeks or months in advance.

Nicole lacks the energy to protest when I tell her to run back to her apartment and grab some overnight supplies so we can stay in the cabin together. She's nearly as docile and mute as Malorie these days. I can't think too much about the mountain of recovery in front of them both or I'll have a nervous breakdown. I just need to keep my head down and help them however I can.

After sneaking into our room to grab an overnight bag without disturbing my sleeping sister, I walk down the path to the left of the restaurant and let myself into cabin five—which features two full sized beds, a small bathroom, and a kitchenette—and retrieve a Firestarter from the cabinet next to the wood burning fireplace. We're somehow nearly halfway through October and the sunny, mild fall days have changed to crisp nights without warning. Once the fire is lit, I pull a bottle of red wine out of my bag and make a silent promise to Lou that I'm only going to let Nicole drink this one night. She deserves it after the week she's had, and I'll be next to her all night, making sure she doesn't overdo it. I scan the TV until I land on a channel airing reruns of *Home Improvement* for the next several hours. It's Nicole's comfort show.

A few moments later, she quietly lets herself into the

cabin. She has a cooler of beer in one hand and a box of tampons in the other.

"I see you packed your overnight bag," I say.

"What else could I possibly need?"

"Oh, I don't know . . . a toothbrush?" I suggest.

She reaches down, opens the small red Igloo cooler, and produces a small Ziploc bag, containing the same toothbrush she's been using for a year.

"Nic, you bought that toothbrush when we were Christmas shopping last year in Marquette."

"Yeah, well, it gets the job done," she says in a solemn tone before collapsing on the couch next to me.

Neither of us speaks for an eternity. She's devastated, and I can't find the words that usually come so easily to me when I'm trying to comfort someone. I silently walk to the kitchen, and when she hears the unmistakable sound of a cork being pulled out of the bottle of wine I brought, she thrusts a weak, celebratory fist in the air without moving her gaze from the floor in front of her.

I give us each a healthy pour of cabernet in the red plastic cups I grabbed from the lodge and sit back down next to her on the couch. Nicole takes a long drink from her cup, sets it on the end table next to her, and puts her head on my shoulder. For the next ten or fifteen minutes, we cry. We cry for Mae, for Malorie, for the Big Rich we thought we knew. When we have no tears left in us, she turns to me, wiping her eyes and prepares for what I think is going to be a revelatory statement.

"You're fucking that podcast dork, aren't you?"

I erupt in laughter. *That's* what's on the top of her mind right now? It's obvious to me she needs an escape; a change of subject, if only for one night.

"No, I'm not, but I think I might like him," I begin, before spending the next hour detailing my evolving feelings for Nolan. Unexpectedly, Nicole seems somewhat accepting of the idea. She doesn't bash him any further than calling him a dork, which is wildly different than her response to any guy I've dated since the eighth grade.

Dougie stops by with food from the restaurant for us, packaged by Lou, and he suggests the idea of staying to join in on our girl's night.

"C'mon, we can have a sleepover like old times," he pleads.

"You wish, you little perv," she tells him before taking the bag of food from his hands, pushing him backward, and gently slamming the door in his face.

After stuffing ourselves with cheeseburgers and fries, Nicole and I watch an old Meg Ryan movie and are both struggling to keep our eyes open by the end credits. We stand next to each other in the ridiculously small bathroom and brush our teeth. We elbow each other to fight for the tiny stream of water while rinsing, just like we did during sleepovers when we were young.

"I love you, KB," she tells me as she climbs into one of the beds and pulls the covers up to her chin.

"I love you, too, Nic. For what it's worth, I know you can't control when horrible things happen, but what you *can* control is how you respond. You and I have both been dealt a shitty hand lately, but I know us. We're going to be okay. We're going to figure it out. We aren't going to let this break us to the point that we can't recover."

She hesitates so long I wonder if she's even going to respond. She leans herself up on one elbow to reach the small lamp on her nightstand and clicks it twice to shut the light off. She inhales, and I prepare for her comeback about me sounding like an after school special.

"I know we're going to be okay, Katie. I'm just tired. I think I just need to rest."

· · ·

When I awake the next morning, I squint through my tired eyes to see that Nicole's bed is empty. I groggily search the room before I notice her sitting in the small breakfast nook next to the window of the cabin, facing the lake. Coffee is brewing and she doesn't have a cup yet, so she must have just woken up as well. She's staring at her phone but not scrolling.

"Morning, dipshit," I groan as I reach down in the sheets to find my warm socks. It's freezing in here, and I'm not sure I have enough wood for a morning fire before we get ready for work.

"It's Nelson," she says, still staring at her phone. Sheriff Nelson has been first in command for Grady PD as long as I can remember. Malorie's case has overshadowed his entire career and now that she's home safe, the assumption is that he will retire soon.

"What could he possibly want this early?"

"They got the toxicology reports back from Mae's autopsy. She died from an overdose of some drug I've never heard of, but Nelson said it's the technical term for sleeping pills. She killed herself, KB. She couldn't stand to be on this earth, knowing what her son did. I'm not sure I've ever felt this heartbroken."

I shudder when I think about how much more heartbreak she'll experience when she finds out what Mae knew. I don't make a habit of lying to Nicole, but I'll be keeping this horrible secret as long as I possibly can.

Eight

WE ARE by no means out of the woods, but Mal seems a little better each time she meets with Dalia this week. I don't know what is discussed during these sessions, but I notice small improvements each time the therapist's car backs out of our gravel parking lot and I'm able to reenter our bedroom.

Last week, Mal started drinking coffee. Monday, she sat out on the balcony with me for an hour during my lodge shift. She barely spoke but I enjoyed it so much, I got a little choked up while asking if she needed a blanket for her legs. She shook her head and refused, but smirked in my direction and nodded her thanks before I took the seat next to her. It was a beautiful, sunny day, and thank goodness there weren't any reporters outside; Mal was able to sit out there until the lunch rush began, and all the arriving cars reignited her anxiety.

Today is Sunday, the week before Halloween, and we are having a family dinner to celebrate Brenda's birthday. Sunday is the slowest night of the week for the restaurant, so we are trusting the off-season employees to run the shift on their own so the family can all eat together in the lodge. Lou is alternating between checking on her pork roast and peeking her head out the windows that overlook the restaurant to make sure they aren't "running the place into the ground," as she has thrice suggested.

"Lou, it's Sunday night and the restaurant is less than a football field's length away. We even have one of the restaurant radios up here if they need us," I remind her.

I pull the white pail of brandy slush mix out of the freezer and begin filling everyone's glasses halfway before topping them off with Sprite. I'm wondering if Mal might want one when my thoughts travel to her spending her twenty-first birthday underground with that lunatic. I could kill him for robbing her of life's most special moments and for robbing us of spending them with her.

Nicole has come out of her funk a little this week and seems to be slowly accepting the fact that Mae took her own life. The first few days were semi-manic, as she repeatedly called Sheriff Nelson and begged him to exhume Mae's body and test for any sort of terminal cancers or illnesses that would indicate she would have died anyway. She had a very hard time stomaching the concept of being cheated out of spending a few more years with her beloved grandmother, and somehow, knowing that she would have died anyway is news that Nicole feels would give her comfort. Nelson assured Nicole that the thorough autopsy would have detected any terminal cancer that Mae had in her body and once again suggested that Nic take some time off and book a session with a grief counselor.

Lou gives me the stink eye when I hand Nicole her drink and I shrug. We're all here at home together and none of us will let Nicole get out of hand. Dad comes out of our bedroom and closes the door behind him. Mal has been opening up to him a lot more this week and even upgraded her response to a non-committal smirk when he invited her to come stay with him in Marquette for the dozenth time. I think she gained a whole new respect for our advantageous father when she found out that he has repeatedly refused increasing dollar amounts to give an interview about Mal's homecoming. "My daughter's story is not for sale and isn't mine to tell. When she feels like talking, that's when you'll hear from us," he repeated each time a different news outlet contacted him.

One of the hardest parts about the intense curiosity from the general public is that I actually get it. I totally understand wanting to know the details. This missing girl who has lived in the back of their minds for twenty years suddenly reemerges, and nobody has a single detail about what she has endured during those two decades. Everyone knows she's alive and seemingly well, with two residents of her hometown arrested for her disappearance. The nation has been guessing what happened to Malorie Rose Benard all these years and now that they know she survived, they've understandably got questions. There were a million and one theories about where Malorie might have been taken that night in 2003, and not one of them were bold enough to assume she was kept right here in Grady. How did she go undetected all those years? Rich is no criminal mastermind; surely there were some close calls, and it's inevitable that he had a little help keeping his dirty secret.

All of us notice but none of us comment when Deb sets a place at the table for Malorie. We've done it for years at each family gathering or holiday celebration, but it's usually a symbolic place setting with a picture of Mal and a few flowers. Now there is a plate, silverware, glass, and napkin because Malorie is alive and, although doubtful, she could technically come out of that room and join us for dinner. If I think about the gravity of it all, the room once again will begin to spin, so I shift my focus to Nicole and Dougie carrying on with their typical badgering of each other.

"I didn't get any texts from you asking for money this year. Does that mean you scrounged up enough to get your mom a gift, or did you just forget altogether?" Nicole asks him before taking her seat next to me and across from Dougie.

"She's lying, mom. I've never asked her for money to buy you a gift," he says to Brenda.

"Well sweetheart, considering the gifts you've given me in the past, maybe you should have," Brenda responds, delivering what may be the first joke I've ever heard her tell at Dougie's expense.

"Brenda!" Nicole exclaims, standing up from her chair to high-five my aunt. "That's what I'm talking about."

"You are slowly poisoning this family," Dougie mumbles before taking a sip of his cocktail.

"Alright, everyone. The food is ready. Please, for the love of God, put the serving utensils on the spoon rests after you make your plate. When you set them directly on the counter, guess who has to clean up that mess every year? Me. That's right. Every damn year I clean up after you ungrateful shits after cooking a feast fit for kings. Use. The. Damn. Spoon rests," Lou announces while grabbing her pack of cigarettes off the table and excusing herself to the balcony. She normally needs one or two after the stress of cooking for all of us.

We form a line at the kitchen island to start filling our plates with a spread so vast it rivals Thanksgiving dinner, while bickering with each other over who the non-spoon rest using culprit is. The consensus is Dougie, thanks to a campaign launched by Nicole detailing all the reasons why he's the most likely suspect. I fall to the back of the line, contently smiling over the realization that this almost feels like a normal family meal. No deaths, nobody is missing, no further arrests, no bombshells. Just my dysfunctional family gathered on a Sunday night in October to celebrate a birthday. If it weren't for the closed door of my bedroom concealing my older sister who was kidnapped for two decades, you might even say it looks like a typical small-town American Sunday night.

I'm so lost in the moment I don't even hear the door open. I simply catch the sight of Malorie grabbing her empty plate from the table and taking her place in line behind me. I mentally plead with every damn person in this room to play it cool. Don't make too big of a deal out of her presence or we will spook her back into the bedroom. I watch each family member's eyes as they take their seat at the table and notice Mal in line to fill her plate. Other than the single tear I see roll down Brenda's cheek before she quickly dabs it with her napkin, everyone is doing great. Lou comes back in through the balcony door and grabs her plate from the table. She takes a spot behind Mal in line and mutters, "I know better than to go behind Dougie when there's mashed potatoes. I hope that little shit left enough for us."

I turn around and see Malorie smiling. A genuine smile. Once our plates are filled, Malorie takes her seat at the table. The same chair she sat in during family meals in high school. She briefly glances at Nicole, who is seated in Mom's old spot, but doesn't seem bothered by it. She wears a content smile as she cuts into her roast and begins to eat the first proper meal I've seen her consume since she arrived home. Until now, it's been Pop Tarts, oatmeal, protein bars, or those cheap little cracker and cheese packs. Before I take my seat, I retrieve her empty glass and mix her up a brandy slush. I'm not sure if she's ever consumed alcohol, so I set a can of Pepsi next to the cocktail in front of her. Pepsi was her drink of choice when we were young.

Everyone pretends not to watch as Mal lifts the glass to her lips and takes a sip. She winces slightly, considers it, and then takes another.

"This isn't so bad. I see why Mom liked them so much," she says. It is the first full sentence she's spoken directly to the family. Although she's made progress with one-on-one meetings in our room and our brief visit out on the balcony, she hasn't spent time in a room with all of us since her rescue. Everyone is holding their breath. I even see Dougie's lip trembling. Brenda is, per usual, the first to lose it and she gasps, slapping her hand over her mouth.

"I'm so sorry, I'm trying to keep it together. I'm just so happy you're here. I'm just so damn happy, Malorie," she cries out. Within seconds, everyone is in tears. Malorie is at our table. She is alive, healthy, and eating a Sunday roast with us. She's drinking a brandy slush, our mom's favorite cocktail. She's talking.

"It's okay, guys," Malorie says. She's making eye contact with us, another thing that hasn't happened much since her return. "I'm happy I'm here, too."

For this one moment, all is right in the world.

Nine

TODAY IS the least Monday-like Monday in the history of Mondays. The late October sun is shining over the calm waters of Grady Lake, and everyone in town is busy preparing for Halloween tomorrow. The entire Benard family is overjoyed with last week's family dinner. Dad, who has now moved back into his home in Marquette, drove down to Grady before the sun came up to make us all French toast. Nicole hasn't insulted Dougie all morning. Malorie turned the TV on in our room for the first time. It's my day off from the restaurant and I have the early lodge shift today, which may not even be necessary for much longer if Mal's condition continues to improve.

Nolan arrives at the lodge just as most of the family is leaving to do morning prep work at the restaurant. He has generously agreed to install security cameras for us at both entrances to the lodge so we won't be as concerned about people trying to snoop around our living quarters. The motion alerts will go to my phone and Lou's phone, as we are the two who wear smart watches and can be notified the quickest.

I invite Nolan upstairs to have some leftover breakfast, and I can sense his hesitation. He still hasn't met Mal. The first episode of his podcast's new season debuted Friday to record-breaking numbers and currently sits at the top of the charts for true crime. It has to be odd to study every painstaking detail about a missing girl and then have the opportunity to meet her.

"I don't think Malorie would want a podcaster in her personal space, Katie," Nolan responds after my invitation.

"Malorie has been underground for twenty years and probably doesn't know what a podcast is, Nolan," I quip.

"Who else is up there?" he asks.

I just watched Brenda and Deb walk with Dougie over to the restaurant. Nicole headed to the Grab N Go to do inventory. My dad is descending the stairs as we speak.

"Should just be Lou," I tell him.

Dad gets down to the landing and gazes up in Nolan's direction, who is currently on a step ladder installing the small white camera over the back entrance to the lodge.

"Nolan, my man! We have some French toast and hashbrowns left upstairs if you're hungry," Dad tells him.

Nolan, ever the gentleman, climbs down from the ladder and shakes my dad's hand.

"Thank you for the offer, sir. It smells delicious, and I might just have to go make a plate when I'm done here."

"Don't wait too long in a house full of hungry women or you'll starve. I learned that the hard way," Dad says, patting him on the back as he carefully passes the ladder to walk to his car. "Have a good day, kids! It's Devil's Night; stay out of trouble."

"Is that still a thing?" Nolan asks me after waving goodbye to Dad and climbing back up the ladder, where he holds out his palm for me to hand him his screwdriver.

"In a town this small, traditions live forever. Also, it's a great day to celebrate. There are no missing girls and Lincoln Palmer is in jail."

"Speaking of Lincoln Palmer, one of my sources told me that Sammie Spencer was offered a check with a lot of zeroes to do a primetime interview, and they apparently are going to try to get Malorie to sit down with her."

"Fat chance of that ever happening. What about the other girl that they rescued from the bunker with Sammie?" I ask him.

He tightens one last screw and then steps back down off the ladder. "I hate to be the bearer of bad news, but it doesn't sound like she's doing too well. They transferred her down to a hospital in Green Bay. They put her in a medically induced coma, but that's all the info I have. They still haven't released her name. My partner and I have scoured online records for minor females who went missing last year from Cincinnati, but there are more names than we could have ever imagined. That might be a story in itself that we need to cover on the podcast," he tells me.

"You know, I saw some article about how Ohio is having an alarmingly large number of children disappearing this year, but I thought it was just clickbait, so I didn't look further into it."

"When I'm done in Grady, Karli and I might head down there and see what we can find out," he says, rubbing his shoulder with his free hand and wincing.

Judging by my internal reaction both to the pain in his shoulder and to the idea of him traveling alone with his female podcast partner, I'd say I'm officially smitten. *How did this happen?*

"If anyone can get to the bottom of it, it's you and Karli," I say with a smile that appears more forced than I intended.

"Her wife texted me this morning and said she's happy for the success we are seeing with the new season, but Karli is cramping her style while she studies for the LSATs and she begged me to take her back out on the road," he says with a casual laugh.

Wife? Yes. Yes. Yes. Nolan can go on the road with that lovely woman all he wants, and I have nothing to worry about. If I had been an earlier follower of their podcast, I probably would have known she had a wife.

"Why don't you take me up on the breakfast offer and we can sneak into Lou's room and steal one of the painkillers she keeps in her bathroom from the knee surgery she had last year?" I suggest.

"Didn't you say she's up there?" he asks, and I laugh when I see the look of apprehension on his face. Every man is terrified of Lou. She's my hero.

"Stealing opiates from Lou Benard is the perfect Devil's Night dare. C'mon, you coward. Let's go," I say with a wink, looping my arm around his uninjured one and leading him up the stairs. "I'm only joking," I whisper when I can see his pulse throbbing through his neck.

"I know," he responds unconvincingly.

"I said no journalists," Lou greets us when we enter the door. She's cleaning my dad's mess from the kitchen counter and packaging leftover toast into a Tupperware container, as if anyone is going to reheat it later. Nolan opens his mouth to apologize, and Lou cracks a smile. "I'm kidding, Nolan. Welcome to our home, and thank you for throwing up those cameras, especially in your condition," she says, jutting her chin toward his injured shoulder.

The phrase *throwing up those cameras* insinuates it was a quick and easy job, but I don't correct her.

"Katie has the login info for the home security app and can show you the basic functions. If either of you have questions, I should be in town for a few more days."

The idea of him leaving puts my stomach in knots. I want

Nolan to get to know the Katie Benard that doesn't have a missing sister, or a missing resort guest, or a dead neighbor that she has a past with. I want him to get to know normal Katie and see if we still click when there's nothing salacious to discuss.

"Let me heat you up a plate," Lou offers and doesn't wait for his response before sticking a plate in the microwave and retrieving a mug from the cupboard for his coffee.

"Thank you, Lou," he says, eyes darting down the hall so quickly I nearly miss it. He hasn't been up here before, but from my stories and all the documents he's poured over about my sister's case, I'm sure he can figure out which room is ours.

I take the mug from Lou's hand and pour Nolan a coffee. I point to the fridge and am about to tell him that we don't have oat milk, but we do have creamer, when he shakes his head violently behind Lou's back. I find it adorable that he *really* doesn't want her to know he takes his coffee with oat milk. Nolan and I each take a seat at the table, and he thanks Lou profusely when she retrieves his plate from the beeping microwave and sets it in front of him with a fork and napkin.

He eats his toast and hashbrowns while installing the camera app on my phone, and it's the quietest moment we've had since the day we met. I'm not sure if he's uneasy because Lou is in the kitchen cleaning or because Malorie Rose Benard is merely steps away from him, or both.

"Those vultures after you for an interview since you cracked the case, kid?" Lou calls from the kitchen.

Nolan briefly chokes on his food before wiping the corners of his mouth with a napkin and coughing briefly. "Yes ma'am, they sure are. I was just telling your niece that the major networks are trying to score an interview with Sammie Spencer and Malorie together, so you may want to avoid your inbox for the foreseeable future."

"My inbox, my phone, my mailbox, they've already tried it

all. Our sweet girl has been gone since 2003; you'd think they'd give us a moment to breathe before hounding us like this," Lou says, scrubbing the same area of the kitchen counter so thoroughly she might soon see her reflection in it.

It's an odd conversation to have with Nolan, who is technically a journalist, but I'm happy to see that Lou hasn't lumped him in with the rest. One of the reasons victims' families have been so willing to work with Nolan on previous cases he's covered is because of his level of respect for their privacy and well-being. He never pushes someone for an interview they don't want to give and never airs audio footage they don't approve. In the episodes I've listened to since we met, I've been quite impressed with the genuine compassion he seems to have for the nightmare these families have found themselves in the middle of.

"I know it's a touchy subject, but have you considered hiring a spokesperson for the family so you don't have to field all these inquiries? I'm sure it is getting exhausting, not to mention irritating," Nolan says, directing the question at both Lou and me.

"Several PR firms have reached out, but I'm fine just using Sheriff Nelson to deliver any messages we'd like the public to hear. It's no skin off my back to ignore these idiots trying to get face time with Mal," Lou tells him.

"Who is trying to get face time with me?"

I once again didn't even hear Mal come out of our room, and now she's standing behind Nolan. I can see that he is trying incredibly hard to play it cool and failing miserably. I conceal my pleasure at the fact that he is visibly sweating. I can see the beads forming on his forehead. In his defense, he's been covering missing persons cases for five years, and this is most likely his first time coming face to face with one of them.

"Every major news network in America. This is Nolan, by the way," I say as casually as my voice will allow.

"Nolan," she says, and any doubts I had about whether she knows who he is are erased.

"Yes, hi Malorie," he says before standing and holding a shaking hand in her direction, thinking better of it, and performing an awkward and clumsy bow. I'm embarrassed *for* him. She puts him at ease by holding her hand out and gently shaking his.

"I hear you helped bring me home. Thank you." She holds his hand while she says this, releasing it when she's done.

"I'm just happy you're home. Everyone is," he tells her.

"Katie talks about you," she says, the corner of her lips playing into a sly smirk.

"No, I don't!" I nearly shout. Malorie and I both smile because I sound exactly like we did as children, always bickering with each other.

"You wouldn't know because you do it in your sleep," she says with a wink before grabbing a bottled water from the fridge and turning on her heels to return to our room.

"She's kidding," I say, the redness climbing up my neck.

"She seems like a real joker," Nolan replies, raising an eyebrow.

"Okay, you two, let's wrap it up. Dalia is coming to meet with Mal in fifteen minutes, and then she wants to meet with you and me Katie," Lou announces, putting her scrub brush away and finally ending her mission to have the cleanest counters in the Midwest.

"I don't need a counselor," I remind her.

"It's not for a session, kid. She wants to talk to us about Mal."

I can't imagine the internal struggle Nolan is having right now with being a friend to me but also a podcaster who has an insatiable need to know every detail of Mal's recovery.

"I've got to get going anyway; I have a lot of editing to do.

Lou, thank you again for breakfast, and you ladies give me a shout if you have any issues with the cameras."

He rinses his plate, places it carefully in the dishwasher, and grabs his keys from the hook next to the door. I smile when my phone buzzes with a notification from the security cameras and it's Nolan sheepishly waving as he leaves the lodge and heads back down to his cabin.

I walk down to our room to remind Mal she has a session with Dalia, and when I enter, she's standing at our window, looking down at the path next to the restaurant where Nolan is walking.

"Do I really say his name in my sleep?" I ask, joining her as we gaze down at the back of his head.

"No, but I wanted him to think that you do. This relationship has to progress soon or I'm going to die of boredom waiting for something to happen."

"Mal!" I playfully slap her arm. "I wasn't sure if you knew."

"Katie, I've been watching you out the window and overhearing your conversations with Dougie and Nicole about him for weeks. I may have been MIA for the last twenty years, but I'm not a complete idiot. I just wish you felt comfortable talking to me about it."

I chuckle.

"Oh, yes, Mal. Welcome home after being kidnapped for the last two decades. Please let me tell you the most insignificant details about my crush on a podcaster."

She doesn't miss a beat before smiling and asking me, "What the fuck is a podcaster?"

Ten

LOU and I once again find ourselves pacing while Dalia and Malorie are behind closed doors. What are they talking about? What could Dalia possibly want to involve Lou and me for? Is she ready to talk about what happened the night she was taken and wants Dalia there to facilitate the conversation?

We look at our watches in unison when a security alert pops up. It's Sheriff Nelson. I can tell by the bald head shining in plain view of our new camera. We hear him climbing the back stairs, and Lou unlocks the door to meet him in the entryway.

"Afternoon, Nelson," she greets the sheriff, who is in full uniform and wearing a grim expression. "I hate to turn you away, but Malorie is in a therapy session and her therapist wants to talk to Katie and me when they are done, which should be any minute."

"That's actually why I'm here," he says, gently pushing past her and taking a seat at the dining room table. "Dalia is going to update you on some information she's gained from Malorie, with Mal's permission of course. I'm giving everyone an update about the case we have against Richard Lowery."

Hearing him call Rich by his full name is jarring. It's incredibly formal and no doubt intentional. He has delayed retirement from the force solely because he couldn't rest until he found out what happened to Mal, and it turns out her captor was under his nose the entire time. They shared beers, they fished together, they even went down to Indiana each year to attend NASCAR races. I can't imagine the shame he feels. Not that he deserves a bit of it—we were all fooled by Richard Lowery, even his own daughter.

Lou and I don't have time to ask any questions before the bedroom door opens and both Dalia *and* Malorie step out. Dalia places a gentle hand on Mal's back and leads her to the three of us, sitting in anticipation at the kitchen table. Dalia nods to Malorie, and Malorie takes a deep breath.

"I want to feel okay again. I want to have as much of my old life back as possible. I want to feel joy again. I've been really overwhelmed because I don't even know where to begin, and every time I think about the last twenty years, I am angry. I'm furious with Rich for stealing the best years of my life."

In the middle of the last sentence, her bottom lip twitches slightly and she shakes it away, visibly angry at herself for getting emotional. As if this isn't the heaviest thing anyone on earth could be dealing with.

"You're here and you're healthy. There's no reason the next years of your life can't be the best. I know we all are going to do whatever we can to make that possible," I tell her, reaching forward to grab her left hand from its resting position on the table. It feels so good to hold the same thin, lanky fingers she had when we were teens.

"I believe that, Katie Bug. I do. I think I just need to work through the anger first and get some things off my chest," she says, and I can tell by the determination in her eyes that she's about to drop some bombs. She turns her head toward Dalia, and the therapist nods. "I need you to know that during the first year of my captivity, I gave birth."

Lou springs to her feet and slaps the table so violently, we all flinch.

"God damn it, Nelson, give me the keys to his cell now. I'm going to fucking kill him. I don't care how much time I get!"

Dalia and Nelson both rise and put their hands on Lou's shoulders, as if they can talk Lou into accepting the fact that Richard Lowery impregnated her niece and gave the baby away to god-knows-who.

"It wasn't Rich's baby," Mal says so quietly, I barely hear her. Her eyes are glistening, and I can promise you she'd rather be talking about anything else in the world. I cannot imagine how painful this is.

"Please sit down and listen to what Malorie is telling you," Dalia says to Lou. Against all odds, Lou listens.

"I know you have a lot of questions, and I'm not sure I have the energy to answer them all. I was told there have been some rumors that I was secretly seeing Bradford Palmer. I wasn't. I was seeing his father, Lincoln. We were in love. Well, what I thought was love."

Lou and I are doing our best not to react and discourage Mal from telling us more. Judging by Nelson's non-reaction, he already knew about Lincoln Palmer. I'm just not sure how long he's known, and for his sake, it better not have been too long, or Lou will strangle him.

"I found out I was pregnant and Lincoln wanted me to get rid of the baby. We had a huge fight about it and then he left town for work without telling me, and I was devastated. I went out to the boon dock to cry and ran into Rich on the way. In a moment of weakness, I told him everything. He said he was going to protect me, and I didn't know what he meant. I hopped on the back of his four-wheeler, willingly, so we could go talk at his cabin. It was the worst mistake of my life."

I might lose my lunch, right here on the table. I was with Benson Palmer on a scratchy picnic blanket, just yards from the old boon dock. I remember being spooked when we heard an engine fire up and he promised me that if we stayed still and low to the ground, nobody would see us. It was too dark. I listened to that asshole, and the engine we heard was Rich taking Malorie. No wonder her DNA wasn't found in his truck when he was questioned that week; she was never in his truck. If she would have just made it a quarter mile deeper into the woods before encountering Rich, she would have run into us. No doubt she would have been furious with me for sneaking out of the woods to make out with Benson, but I could have ditched him and sat on the dock with her. She could have told me everything. I can't believe we were so close when she was taken. It's a strange feeling knowing one decision could have changed everything. I wonder how many situations happen in our lives that would have been so drastically different with one left turn instead of a right. I can't even be angry with Benson anymore; he's gone now, too. I'm only angry with myself. And Rich.

All the conversations I've had with Dougie and Nicole over the years, speculating about what could have happened to Mal play rapidly through my mind. Me complaining that Mal had been in a foul mood for weeks. Dougie suggesting that maybe she was involved with someone older that we never would have suspected. It was all right in front of us.

"The baby didn't make it," Mal says, and the tears break free from her eyes in a steady stream. "I'm not surprised; I had no prenatal care at all. I never ate anything but processed foods and didn't see daylight for months."

Nelson cuts in.

"The crime scene techs are still doing organized digs on

several of Rich's properties, but there are a lot of acres to comb, and it could take months, not considering the time they'll have to pause when the ground is frozen. Rich told Malorie he buried the baby on the property, but he didn't say which property. I promise your entire family, I will not retire until we find him or her and give that baby a proper burial."

"Him or her? He wouldn't even tell you the sex?" I ask.

Mal shakes her head. "The pain was so bad. It was indescribable. I think I even blacked out a few times. I kept asking why the baby wasn't crying. Rich had my baby wrapped in an old shower curtain. I just kept thinking about how the baby deserved more than a burial in a decades-old shower curtain from Rich's musty guest bathroom. He told me it would only make it harder for me to grieve if I knew the sex. A few years later, he was drinking and referred to her as a she, but I don't know if he was just playing mind games on me. It would mean the world to me if we could bury her next to Mom."

"Of course, sweetheart. Of course, we will. She will have the most beautiful headstone in the whole county," Lou assures her. "Nelson is going to make sure we find her."

Nelson clears his throat. "We have a list of offenses that Richard Lowery will be formally charged with, but sexual assault will not be among the charges."

My and Lou's heads both snap toward Malorie, involuntarily. Lou tries to recover by explaining herself.

"Sweetie, that's a huge relief to hear, trust me. But are you sure?"

Malorie nods solemnly.

"I know the entire world assumes that was Rich's motivation behind kidnapping me and why they also assume Lincoln was involved. Rich is sick in the head and honestly believed he was protecting me from Lincoln, because he knew what kind of guy he was. He was convinced that Lincoln would eventually find me and the only way to prevent that was to make him think I either ran away or that someone else took me. He made me believe he felt it was his duty to do that . . . because he was my biological father."

There is no willpower strong enough to prevent Lou and I from gasping. Nelson holds his hands up before we can start asking questions. "Now, we know that to be a lie. With the DNA your mother and Chuck provided years ago and the hair samples we took from Malorie's personal belongings, there's never been a doubt that Chuck is your father. We still aren't sure what led Rich to believe he could have been Malorie's dad, and he's not talking yet."

"Does Dad know this yet?" I ask.

"Yes, I spoke with him this morning, and then drove straight here. Malorie thought it would be best if he was told separately."

"How did he take it?" Lou asks.

"As expected," Nelson replies, and we all understand that means he's currently drinking himself into oblivion.

"I think that's probably enough for today, right Malorie?" Dalia asks, placing a gentle hand on her shoulder.

"I have one last question. I need to know . . . where was Mom when she had her heart attack? Who was she with?" Malorie asks. Her hands are shaking. The look on Dalia's and Nelson's faces tells me this isn't a subject they've discussed.

"She was leaving the Grab N Go and walking the trail back to the resort. Mae saw her go down and called 911. Why?" Lou asks.

"There's something else you need to know," Malorie says, and now her entire body is shaking.

Part Two

Eleven

FALL 1999

THE MAN nervously flicks the lid to his silver custom engraved lighter open and closed several times while he paces the empty lakeside lot.

"I don't know, Lincoln. It sounds like a lot of risk doing this here in Grady, especially since you're planning on planting roots here."

He gives a smile, one that only Lincoln Palmer can give, the one that somehow charms whoever he is speaking with into believing whatever bullshit he is about to spew. It's worked for him since he was a boy.

"First of all, it's a foolproof plan. The bunkers will be on Rich Lowery's empty land. Second, I'm a millionaire philanthropist. Believe me when I say I am the last person on anyone's mind when it comes to missing girls from the wrong side of the tracks. I could snatch one in broad daylight and I wouldn't make the suspect list."

The man turns the lighter a few times in his hand. It was a gift from Rich when he stood in his wedding to Nicole's mother. It was such a beautiful spring wedding by the lake and no one in attendance could have imagined it would end with Rich becoming a widower and single dad of one, less than three years later, when his bride died during the birth of their only child.

"Yeah, and what if Rich gets curious?" the man asks.

"I am paying him a lot of money not to be curious. Plus, I have him convinced that I'm growing pot in the bunkers, and I'm supplying him with plenty of it for his ailments. He told me the less he knows, the better, and I couldn't agree more. You'll never be associated anyway; he thinks I just met you when I bought land in Grady."

The man continues to pace.

"Look, Palmer, I don't plan on doing this forever. I know it's a sickness. I can't keep this up."

Palmer smiles.

"And when you say you're done, you're done. No hard feelings."

"How do I know you're not going to kill me so I don't get you locked up?" he asks.

"Well, I have a little insurance. A polaroid from Detroit."

The man's head jerks up. "Polaroid? A picture? How the fuck—"

"You got sloppy and drank too much. I snapped a pic of you passed out with that girl from Woodward. I know you're a family man, and I had to have something in case you went soft and flipped on me. Don't be mad, friend. It's only business."

"And what insurance do I have?" he asks, shoving the lighter into his pocket.

"You don't. Which is why you aren't going to go soft on me."

"And this girl now, the one you've decided to parade around in front of everyone? I'm a risk to you, but somehow she isn't?"

Lincoln pulls his hand out of the pocket of his dress pants and waves his ring finger in the air. "We eloped. Now she has several million reasons to never complain about anything in life. Besides, I basically pulled her out of the gutter with the life she was living. She should be thanking me."

"And when a woman named Ashley Smith who has a missing person's report filed for her suddenly appears in Grady, Michigan—how are you going to explain that?"

Lincoln taps the side of his temple with his finger and smirks. "She called her parents last week to let them know she's safe and sound and they called the local police to let them know and cancel the report. I told her she could have a whole new life up here; I even let her pick out a new name. Would you believe the bitch picked *Fallon*? The boys already hate her, so she's fitting right in as a stepmom."

Twelve

FALL 2002

SAME PACING, same lighter cap being flipped open and closed, same deliberations over whether he should be partnering with Lincoln Palmer or simply bowing out and getting help for his addictions.

He's on Rich Lowery's vacant land, the land that now conceals two bunkers and the scattered remains of several young women, which is something the man does *not* have anything to do with. He wants no part in killing young women; that's a sickness that belongs to Lincoln Palmer, and he refuses to be anywhere near that monster when he takes their lives.

Today, he's headed down to the first bunker to bring food and water to Elizabeth, the sixteen-year-old that Palmer inexplicably took from Milwaukee last week. He's still not sure what the fuck that maniac was thinking. Taking her in the middle of the day with no assistance was risky and stupid. He can't believe Palmer didn't get caught. Bringing her food and water will be all the man is doing, as Elizabeth is young enough to be his daughter. Palmer is out of town yet again for work so he's the girl's only lifeline for staying alive all week while he's away.

He scans the woods a few times before lifting the trap door to expose the concrete steps down to the steel door of the bunker. When the coast is seemingly clear, he takes a few steps down and unlocks the steel door before turning around to retrieve the bottled water and loaf of bread he set on the stairs. When his back is turned, an elbow comes down on the back of his skull with such force, you'd never imagine it came from a teenage girl.

His knees hit the stairs first, followed by his chin when his brain doesn't react quickly enough for his arms to fly forward and soften the fall. The girl climbs over his back in the narrow stairwell and runs toward the light of day showing through the trap door that is still wide open.

"Help! Help me! Somebody! Help!" she shrieks.

The man gains his bearings, climbs up the stairs and grabs the girl's delicate ankle with his oversized right hand just before she can clear ground level and make a run for it. She screams again, but this time it's muffled by the noise of her head hitting the side of the stairwell when he yanks her back down. Within minutes, the trap door is closed, the girl is once again secured in the bunker, and the loaf of bread and bottled water are angrily tossed in the corner, mere feet from the bucket she uses as a bathroom.

"You nearly just cost yourself your life, young lady. I wouldn't fucking try that again," he tells her, spitting on the ground next to where she sits.

She's sobbing now, but something about the chemical makeup in the man's brain is trained to feel absolutely nothing when females cry and beg for mercy.

Above ground, it's a beautiful autumn day with overcast skies and a light wind that is shaking loose the gold and crimson leaves from the trees above the bunker. Less than thirty feet from the trap door, doing his best to slow his heartrate and quiet his haggard breathing from what he just witnessed on his own land, is Richard Lowery. This is the day Rich realizes that Lincoln is doing more than growing marijuana on his land, and he's not doing it alone.

Thirteen

FALL 2003

FOR AN ENTIRE YEAR, Rich has been aware that Lincoln Palmer is doing the unthinkable, and it's happening beneath the ground of the beautiful lakeside lot he worked so hard to save up for. It's happening less than two hundred yards from the dock his daughter has jumped off every summer since she could swim, and not even a mile from the business that, until now, was keeping his family afloat. The Grab N Go hasn't *really* paid the bills in years, a secret he has been ashamed to share with his only family in this world—his mother, Mae and daughter, Nicole. Now they are all surviving on hush money, and the two women haven't the slightest clue. Nicole happily clocks in for her after-school shifts, stocking shelves or working as cashier. Mae lives her retired life of leisure sitting in a white rocking chair outside the store and gossiping with the locals. Rich hasn't slept a full night in years.

He spends most sleepless nights preparing his doomsday room, a midsize cellar behind a soundproof wall in the basement of his cabin. When he built the room, it was a space to bring his family in case of an atomic bomb, a home invasion, an airborne plague. Now it's the room where he'll hide when Lincoln Palmer finally finds out just how much Rich knows about his misdeeds and comes for him.

Luckily, Palmer is out of town this week for one of his *business trips*. Judging by the footage from the hidden trail cam Rich installed in a stack of firewood where Lincoln typically parks when he comes to the land, he likes to bring trophies back from his trips. He hasn't seen Lincoln's partner in crime all year, not since the day Rich saw the girl trying to escape from one of the underground bunkers. Rich has known the man his entire life and prays every night that he's been absent because he has come to his senses. He wants to tell him he knows. He wants *so badly* to grab him by the shoulders and shake him. But each time he sees him, he freezes up and changes his mind when he considers the implications of knowing about the girl for a year and not reporting it. He'd probably spend years in prison.

Tonight, shortly after midnight, Rich parks his truck at the Grab N Go and hops on his four-wheeler, driving deep into his not-so-empty land. A little over a mile through the woods, and off the only trail on the property, is a small box built into an old oak tree. Rich reaches into his back pocket, retrieves his wallet, and pulls out a small key for the lockbox. When he opens it, he sees a fat white envelope. The same envelope that awaits him each month, so he'll keep his mouth shut. Since early 2000, he's kept his promise. For the last twelve months, a healthy chunk of the money is spent on bourbon so Rich can drown that screaming girl out of his racing thoughts and attempt to get a few hours of sleep.

He takes the trail on his way back to the store, mostly so he can steal a view of the lake. The lake his parents built their convenience store on and made a life for themselves so little Richard Lowery could carry on their legacy. How has he done that? By harboring fugitives and turning a blind eye to a kidnapped girl. His father would be real proud.

When he's nearly back to the store, he sees young Malorie Benard on the trail, walking toward the old boon dock. He kills the engine. Even when she's crying, she's beautiful. She is the spitting image of her mother, Beth, at that age. Rich had a few fun nights with Beth when they were teenagers and, truth be told, one *very* special night with her early in her marriage to Chuck when she stumbled into the Grab N Go three sheets to the wind after they'd had a big fight. Rich himself was a newlywed and was consumed with guilt over his lust-filled tryst in the back of his old Dodge pickup.

"Malorie Benard, what are you doing out at this hour?" he asks, hopping off the side of his ATV.

Malorie is rapidly sniffing to quell her tears, but she's unsuccessful. She only cries harder as Rich approaches and tugs at her long brown ponytail, trying to make her smile. It doesn't work.

"I'm just having a really hard night, Big Rich. Life isn't fair sometimes."

He gives a low whistle. "Boy, is that an understatement. Just when you think you have life figured out, it knocks you around again."

She gives him a sympathetic smile and it nearly knocks him over. He's not quite sure how he's never noticed before this moment. Maybe it's because he stays busy and doesn't pay too much mind to the Benard kids. Maybe it's because he sees her little sister Katie a lot more since she's joined at the hip with Nicole. But tonight, he finally sees it. That crooked smile, the slightly upturned nose? She looks just like *his* mother, Mae. It's not the bourbon playing tricks on him; this girl is no doubt a Lowery.

He tries to listen to her as she pours her little teenage heart out about some boy who has her all bent out of shape, but he's distracted with mental calculations of his adulterous tryst with Beth Benard and how it could have resulted in a beautiful baby girl nine months later. He remembers Beth working the lunch shift at Benards, her round belly nearly knocking over his milkshake as she set it on the table in front of him. He remembers the shame he felt for having Chuck David's wife underneath him for hours, though he felt zero shame while it was happening. He was a married man and she a married woman. It went against everything he ever believed in. But did the dates line up? He remembers it was late summer because his wife was at the State Fair in Escanaba with her sisters that night. She packed a bag and told him she would just stay with one of the sisters in town so she didn't have to drive after having a few beers.

"How old are you now?" he asks her, completely oblivious to the fact that he just cut off a sobbing teenager from her story of heartbreak and betrayal.

"Eighteen. I'll be nineteen in the spring. Why do you ask?"

Spring. That's when she'd have the baby if she got pregnant in late summer. Malorie Rose Benard is his daughter. He's alone now and so is Beth Benard. This could be their second chance. They could be a family. This is the good news he's been waiting for after a year of torture. He knew his life was destined to be great, after all.

"No reason. Now, what were you going on about? Some boy?"

Malorie's tears return. "No, that's what I'm telling you Rich. He's not a boy. But I'm in love. We're in love. Please don't tell anyone. Please. My parents can't know yet. I'm not ready to tell them. I just need someone to talk to, so please just tell me what you think I should do."

"About what?" he asks.

"The baby, Rich. The baby. Haven't you listened to a

word I've said?" she asks, her left hand rising to instinctively cover her not-yet-existent bump.

His eyes travel to her stomach. Pregnant? No, she's just a child herself. She can't raise a baby.

"You're pregnant? Who is the father, Malorie?"

She hangs her head, shaking it slowly. She can't look him in the eyes.

"Malorie, sweetheart, I'm not going to tell your mother. But if I'm going to help you, you have to tell me who the father is so we can handle this."

"Rich . . . it's . . . it's Lincoln Palmer. He loves me."

Rich doesn't remember much of the night after this moment. He only remembers seeing red.

Fourteen

DECEMBER 2004

RICH SITS in a booth across from Beth Benard. She's aged a million years in the fourteen months since Malorie disappeared from her life, and he's wanted to tell her so many times that she's safe. She's okay. She may scream and kick and complain, but he knows it's all an act. She's happy he is protecting her from Lincoln Palmer. She has a roof over her head, food in her stomach, and a warm bed to sleep in. What more could their daughter want? He just had to lay low for a while until the heat was off him before he could involve Beth.

Tonight, as they silently stare at their half-eaten plates at the greasy diner they've been going to for decades, Rich has a gift for the woman he loves. He's going to give her renewed hope. He's going to show her it's not too late to have a happy ending. They can be a family. Once they are married, Nicole and Katie will be sisters. Is there better news for two best friends than finding out they get to be sisters?

They are going to have to work together with Malorie on a story about where she's been all year, but he's already formulated a few ideas. The entire nation will rejoice when she comes home, but it won't be to that cramped lodge with the rest of the Benards; it will be upstairs in the cabin where she currently lives. There are four bedrooms, more than enough room for everyone.

"I have a gift for you," he tells Beth, pulling an envelope out of the inside pocket of his Carhart jacket.

"Oh, Rich. I'm not celebrating Christmas anymore. I can't celebrate much of anything with my baby gone."

Our baby, he thinks. And she'll find out shortly that Malorie isn't gone at all. He slides the envelope across the table and nods for her to open it.

"I think this gift will give you reason to celebrate again," he tells her with a wink. He can hardly contain his excitement. The winter storm that TV6 has been predicting for days is finally kicking into gear, and the giant flakes are beginning to accumulate on the windows of the diner next to their booth.

"It's really starting to come down out there. How about I open it in the car? We really should head back to Grady before the roads get bad."

Rich likes this idea. It's such a personal gift, and maybe it *would* be better if it were opened while they are alone. She's going to be so happy; she'll probably want to jump into his arms, and they don't need the whole county talking about it before they have a chance to announce their love to the world. The dark cab of his truck is a much better place.

He gives Beth a warm smile before paying the bill and standing to assist her with buttoning up her winter coat. She's mildly uncomfortable with his overly sweet demeanor tonight but far too exhausted to fight it. She's too exhausted to do much of anything these days.

He's basically skipping as they walk to his truck underneath the lampposts in the diner's parking lot, which is beginning to look like a giant snow globe. Today is going to be the first day of the rest of his life. *Their* life. He opens the truck door for her, runs around to his side, shakes the snow off his sleeves, and starts the engine with the heater on full blast so Beth won't be cold for long. She's shivering, but darn if she doesn't look adorable doing it. Malorie has grown so much this year and she's looking more like Beth every single day. What a beautiful family he is going to have.

He once again hands her the gift and prepares for her reaction. He hasn't felt intense anticipation like this since the night he proposed to his late wife.

Beth slides her slim index finger under the flap of the red envelope and breaks the seal. She pulls out a card with two penguins on the front and a cheesy Christmas quote about how they mate for life. When she opens the card, a polaroid picture falls from it and lands in her lap, face down. She looks at Rich, confusion on her face. He is smiling, motioning for her to flip it over. When she does, she stares for what seems like an eternity, placing a hand on the dashboard of his truck to steady herself.

"Well, isn't this great news?" he asks, and she promptly opens the door and vomits up everything she just ate at the greasy diner, all over the freshly fallen snow.

The picture is of her daughter, who has been missing for over a year. Her hair is short, in a style Malorie would never wear. She's sitting on a mattress and staring at the ground. She's lost at least ten pounds from her already thin frame.

"Rich . . . what . . . what the fuck is this? Is this some sort of sick joke? Is this my baby?"

Rich reaches over and places his dry, cracked hand on Beth's thigh.

"Let me take you to her."

Fifteen

MALORIE IS fast asleep when she is awoken by the commotion upstairs. Someone is running. The steps aren't heavy enough to be Rich. *Please, God, don't let him have taken another girl*, she thinks. She'd spend another year down here alone if it meant another girl didn't have to suffer the same fate.

She hears the door being lifted, footsteps coming down the stairs, followed by a series of clicks, unlatching the locks from outside the room where she sleeps. She doesn't quite believe it when the door opens and two figures are standing in the opening, backlit by the unflattering bulbs scattered across the basement ceiling. As usual, it's Rich, but beside him is her mother. Her mother, who she hasn't seen in fourteen months. She only knows it's been this long because she started keeping track of the days two months ago when Rich let her know she had officially been "with him" for a year. "Today marks one year that I've kept you safe from that bastard Lincoln Palmer," he'd boasted.

"Mom?" she asks, barely above a whisper. She's tired, disoriented, and convinced that speaking any louder will wake her from whatever dream this must be.

"My baby!" Beth shrieks, running to Malorie.

She hugs her daughter so tightly, Malorie thinks her bones might break. She can't remember the last time someone even touched her. It might have been Mae, the first time she came into the room and saw that Rich was in fact keeping the posterchild for missing girls in America right there in a safe room tucked into his basement. Mae had tried rubbing Malorie's back before the girl shied away and scooted far enough across the mattress to put her back up against the concrete wall. If Mae wasn't there to save her, she didn't deserve to console her.

"Mom, please take me home. I want to go home," Malorie repeated over and over through her sobs.

"Yes, sweetheart, I'm taking you home," she told her, stroking her short hair before pulling away to get a good look at her oldest daughter.

"Do you like her haircut? I had Mae style it just like yours. She looks more like you every day," Rich says to Beth. He's leaning in the doorway with an unmistakable look of pride on his face.

"Rich, what the fuck have you done?" Beth says to him. "Do you know what you've done?"

By now, Malorie has heard Rich rant about how he just wants them to be a family about eighty-seven times. By the second or third day of captivity, it really began to sink in that Rich is mentally ill and does an incredibly fine job of hiding it in public. He's always been a man of few words, which must aid in the process of keeping his delusions a secret.

"Yes, I kept our daughter safe from Lincoln Palmer, and now you're here so we can be a family. There's more than enough room for the three of us here. You can move out of the lodge. Katie can come, too, if she wants," he suggests.

Beth's hands are shaking, and Malorie wants to tell her "No, no, no, Mom. Don't do it. You have to play along. This man is mentally unstable and has an entire arsenal of guns in the house. You have to play along until we can get out of here. Please." But Rich is just feet from them, ready to pounce. Malorie squeezes her mother's hand, her best method of communicating with her to stop, but it doesn't work. Beth Benard is finally confronting the monster who has been keeping her daughter in his basement, and she is absolutely feral. She hasn't slept a full night in over a year. Nearly all her savings have been given to psychics and mediums who promised to tell her what happened to her daughter. She's smoked two packs a day since the night Malorie disappeared. Her other daughter, Katie, is essentially raising herself because Beth doesn't have it in her to be a mother right now. All because of this fucking man.

"Get out of my fucking way, Rich. I'm taking my daughter home."

"*Our* daughter," he corrects her. "And this is her home now. And yours, too."

"What are you talking about? She's not your daughter, Rich. Why would you think that?"

"The night we made love in my truck outside the Grab N Go. It was nine months before she was born. Look at her face, she's my daughter. You can't deny it anymore."

Malorie involuntarily flinches when Rich references making love to her mother, and Beth doesn't immediately deny it. She has assumed Rich was a delusional maniac this entire time, but could it be possible that he actually is her father? Has he been telling the truth this whole time?

"Rich, look at me. Yes, I made a drunken mistake when Chuck and I weren't doing too well, but that was not nine months before Malorie was born. It was *a year* and nine months. Malorie is not your daughter. Now move, so I can get my daughter home."

Beth leans down and grabs a blanket off the mattress behind them and wraps it around Malorie's shoulders. She leads her toward the door, stopping when Rich doesn't move. He reaches behind his back and pulls a handgun from his waistband, pointing it at the women.

"Nobody is going anywhere," he tells them. His eyes have turned black. He's not the same man who was just staring longingly at Beth over their hot plates at the twenty-four-hour diner. A darkness has taken over.

Malorie feels her mother's hand grow cold and clammy before loosening its grip and falling to her side. There's no way she's giving up; they need to get out of here. This is her one chance at freedom. She has to see Katie again. Her real father. Her aunts. Her bedroom. Even her stupid cousin, Dougie. She wonders if Michigan State will still honor the scholarships she had been awarded, a year later. Plenty of students take a gap year, right? She turns to her mother and sees beads of sweat beginning to form at her hairline.

"Mom?" she whispers.

"I don't feel so good, baby," Beth tells her before collapsing into the small blue plastic chair by the door. It's the only place to sit, other than the mattress on the floor.

"Mom? What's wrong?" Malorie asks with urgency, dropping to her knees on the hard cement floor before her.

"I feel a little dizzy and hot," Beth tells her, but her speech is beginning to slur, and Malorie has a hard time understanding her.

"Rich, she's sick. We have to get help," Malorie pleads.

Rich lowers his gun but doesn't move from the doorway. He stares at Beth as she slumps lower into the chair, one hand over her chest and the other reaching for Malorie.

"The Lord decides who shall be punished for their sins; it's not our job to question it," he says, completely void of emotion. Rich backs out of the doorway, closes the steel door, and latches every bolt. Malorie screams for help for so long, she's not even sure it's her voice anymore that she's hearing. It may have been fifteen minutes, but it also could have been two hours. Time no longer existed in the small, windowless room where Malorie held her mother in her arms as she eventually stopped gasping for air and fell unconscious, before dying of what Mal would later learn was cardiac arrest. Her hopes of ever being rescued died with her mother on that dark, blustery winter's night.

Sixteen

JANUARY 2005

MALORIE WASN'T sure how Rich and Mae pulled it off, but they did. The bastard even brought her the obituary from the Grady Gazette, haphazardly throwing it on the ground next to her mattress. Beth Benard died tragically on a snowy evening in December, with the services taking place after the holiday. The article even listed Malorie as a survivor, along with the rest of the family. She could only imagine what her father and Katie were going through. Surely, they thought that Malorie could be dead, and now her mother was gone, too. She's not sure if Rich poisoned her mother or if it was legitimately cardiac arrest from her many bad habits mixed with shock from that night, but she's certain her mother's body was cold by the time Rich and Mae came to retrieve it in the middle of the night. If they'd staged it to look like a heart attack, there's little chance anyone would doubt it enough to order an autopsy, especially in a small town like Grady. Beth Benard smoked like a chimney, never turned down a ribeye steak, and was panic-stricken waiting for her daughter to come home. Nobody would be surprised to hear her poor heart just gave out.

Since Rich's dream of having a family died, so did his desire to treat Malorie like a daughter. The first fourteen months of her captivity, Rich was kind and thoughtful when it came to her living conditions. Well, as kind and thoughtful as someone can be while holding them prisoner in a darkened room. Once he realized that she was indeed Chuck David's daughter, the preferential treatment came to a screeching halt. Gone was the small TV and the collection of DVDs, the down comforter, and the mini fridge. She no longer had a choice of snacks, drinks, and entertainment. She ate what he gave her, and it was usually worse than the meals she was forced to eat at Grady High.

There were many days Malorie was convinced Rich was going to kill her. What good was she to him now? Especially the nights that he drank heavily. He'd come down to her room, usually wielding a pistol, and pace back and forth for what seemed like hours. He would mumble to himself, mostly indecipherable to Malorie, before giving up and slamming the door on his way out. She often wasn't fed for a day or so after these events.

In the twenty years Malorie was hidden away from the rest of the world, there were several times that Rich told her he was bringing her home and even loaded her into his pickup truck before changing his mind. Once he handed her his phone to call her sister, Katie, on her birthday and thought better of it, snatching the iPhone out of Malorie's hands before she could figure out how to place a call on a device she'd never seen before. He let her upstairs under his supervision a handful of times over the years, and she once caught a local news segment covering her case on the tenth anniversary of her disappearance. She was confused by everyone referring to her as Malorie Rose Benard. Nobody used her full name unless she was in trouble. Her heart broke when the newscaster said her sister, Katie, refused to comment or participate in the broadcast, citing her request for privacy. She was twenty-five years old now, and Malorie would have given anything to see how she had grown. Rich would often tell Malorie that Katie and Nicole were outside for bonfires the night before, but she's certain they were just little white lies he told to torture her however he could.

On the nights Malorie would allow herself to dream of being rescued, she was always confronted with the possibility that everyone would ask her why she didn't try harder to escape. He let her upstairs, he let her walk to his truck, he handed her a phone. Why didn't she take advantage of these moments? But the world didn't know Richard Lowery. He's no genius, but he's certainly an expert in emergency preparedness. It's why the small bunker room in his basement exists. It's why it was stocked with enough food and water to keep her alive for weeks when she first arrived. Not only does Rich have an ample supply of guns and ammunition, but he taunted her with the stories of how he installed trip wire all over his acreage so that if she ever decided to run, she'd be dead before she got off the property. He'd come downstairs with stories of seeing Katie at the Grab N Go and how much he'd enjoy taking her out with a sniper rifle as punishment if Malorie ever attempted to escape. There were a million and one reasons why Malorie "didn't try harder" to get out of Rich Lowery's basement.

As silly as it sounds, Malorie was relieved to be brought to his cabin after her first few days of captivity, in which she was kept somewhere underground. She remembers the conversation with him in the woods on his vacant land where she foolishly confessed to being pregnant with Lincoln Palmer's child. She remembers agreeing to get on the ATV with him, and that's pretty much where her memory stops. The next thing she knew, she was waking up in a dark, cold shipping container with a large lump on the side of her head. No food, no water, no light, no sound. After feeling around, she took inventory of the only items surrounding her—a mattress, a bucket, a roll of toilet paper. Her repeated screams only echoed inside her chamber and went unheard to the outside world.

The early days of Malorie's ordeal were spent wondering if her college roommate had been assigned yet, if she'd missed Jenna Joraski's epic graduation party, if Katie was wearing her favorite sweatshirt. Over the years, her thoughts evolved to wondering if anyone still missed her at all.

Seventeen

FALLON PALMER REACHED her breaking point; one she should have reached years ago. She no longer wanted to think of herself as Fallon; she wanted to go back to simply being Ashley. All the money in the world wasn't worth a life like this.

She knows he killed Benson. Lincoln Palmer killed his own son. She's not sure how he did it, or if he even did the dirty work himself, but she has no doubt that Benson is dead because of his father. He figured it out, and because of that, he paid with his life. She's certain the boys have suspected something for years. They have known their father is an asshole since they were old enough to form their own thoughts, but adding rapist and murderer to the list must be a hard pill to swallow when you're talking about your own parent.

What does she have to lose now? Half the town saw her with a bruised face at Benson's funeral. She purposely went easy on the makeup Lincoln threw toward her before they left the house. She can't live another day under his control. She can barely breathe thinking about the girls he has under-ground. She's not sure how many he keeps these days, but she's certain the list includes the missing girl from Benard's Lakeside Inn. How stupid can this man be to take a girl from Grady Lake? When he gets caught, it will be nobody's fault but his own. He got greedy and made a foolish mistake.

Ashley dreams of filing for divorce and returning home to her parents. Over the years, the dreams became plans. She could have her name back and her old life, the one that existed before she was addicted to drugs and foolishly got involved with Lincoln Palmer. She's clean now, and she can start her life over. Her mind is made up—she's leaving. But before she goes, she needs to free the girls.

Chelsey, the head of housekeeping at Palmer's Resort, is Ashley's only friend. She's the only one who knows the truth —the entire truth—about Ashley's past. Chelsey lives in a small cottage on the property, which she thinks is a perk of the job, but Ashley knows better. Lincoln wants his employees on call at any hour, and building a few cabins on the property so they can be at his beck and call is a control game that he's gotten very good at playing.

For the last three months, Ashley has been bringing items to Chelsey's cabin to plan her getaway. A pair of pants here, a few dollars there—it's going to add up to a new life soon. She's also slowly been taking valuable items from their home that she knows Lincoln won't miss so she can sell them later. Much like the other residents of this small town, Chelsey doesn't lock her door, so it's easy for Ashley to slip in, pull the duffle bag out from under her bed, and fill it with another item each day. Lincoln has given Ashley an "allowance" for years of three hundred dollars a week, and the entirety of that allowance has been stockpiled in the inside zippered pocket of her bag for months.

Today is the day. Ashley is going to free the girls, and

Chelsey will be waiting on the main road to drive her to Marquette, where she will catch a flight downstate. She will go back to her old life and never look back. There may be a special reservation in hell for her for staying quiet all these years while her husband abused countless girls, but maybe she'll be shown a spot of mercy for saving a few of them before she goes.

She pulls the duffle bag out one last time, tucking it under the backseat in Chelsey's small sedan.

"Are you sure you want to do this?" Chelsey asks her.

"I *need* to do this," Ashley answers. "Thank you for being my only friend. Once I'm safe, I'll find a way to contact you and let you know."

Chelsey nods and hugs her friend. Ashley isn't sure what will happen to Chelsey's job when the girls escape and Lincoln is arrested, but she's a hard worker, so surely can find a job anywhere. Preferably for an employer who isn't a psychopath.

After her walking shoes are laced up tight, Ashley takes one last look at the life she's leaving behind—a beautiful lakeside resort, hired help at her service, a luxury fleet of vehicles, and a wardrobe that would put the Real Housewives to shame. She's also leaving behind a man who began their relationship by drugging and kidnapping her, a life of lies and abuse, and the loneliest existence imaginable. Other than Chelsey, her only "friends" have been the followers of her ridiculous Instagram account, where she made her life seem impossibly perfect with her posts of beautiful sunsets, expensive trips, and luxurious spa days.

Ashley takes the walking trail around the lake and veers off to an rough, unpaved path when she gets close to Rich Lowery's vacant land, where she knows the girls are kept. For twenty years, Lincoln has sworn up and down that he isn't holding Malorie Benard in either of the bunkers, but Ashley still wonders if she's about to get the surprise of her life when she opens that heavy door. She can't imagine what Malorie would even look like after two decades in a bunker with no light. Her instincts tell her that it's unlikely, only because Lincoln doesn't tend to hold back when he's boasting about his conquests, and he also doesn't tend to keep the girls around that long. If he took Malorie, he would have rubbed it in Ashley's face. Oddly enough, she remembers Lincoln seeming quite distraught when the news of Malorie's disappearance spread. Ashley was surprised; she didn't even know that Lincoln knew Malorie, let alone well enough to be concerned of her whereabouts. He even donated ten thousand dollars to the search efforts. Ashley doesn't plan on seeing Malorie's face when she gets to the bunker, but it sure is fun to dream of being the one to finally find her.

She's mere feet from the trap door entrance to the first bunker. There's no turning back now. Ashley surveys her surroundings before lifting the door, its handle mostly concealed under a patch of artificial grass and fallen leaves. She slowly descends the stairs until she gets to the steel door with a keypad. She enters 0-1-0-9, Lincoln's birthday. The lock makes a loud click.

"Girls, you're going to be okay. I'm coming to free you," she announces, in case one of them is hiding in a corner ready to attack Lincoln.

She opens the door. Nothing. Maybe they are tied up? She pulls the flashlight out of her sweatshirt pocket and clicks it on. Light illuminates the storage container and, aside from some supplies, it is empty. No girls. Ashley exhales and turns to go, leaving the door unlocked and slightly ajar as she leaves. She wants it to be as easy as possible for the police to search for evidence when they arrive. As she ascends to ground level, she decides to close the trap door so that nobody falls into the opening when they arrive at the property. If she's not around to show them where it is, she'll draw a map.

Ashley walks one hundred yards to the next door. This

one is covered with fallen leaves and debris, which makes her wonder how long it's been since Lincoln checked on these girls. She repeats her steps—propping open the door, descending the steps, entering the code, announcing her arrival. This time, she's met with a female voice.

"Who are you?"

"My name is Fall—er—Ashley. My name is Ashley, and I'm here to save you. We have to move quick."

Her flashlight is still illuminated from her trip to the first bunker. She scans the room and sees two other girls. One of them appears to be in bad shape; she's lying on the bed, emaciated and gray. The other is standing, and Ashley stops in her tracks when she realizes it's the girl from the missing posters—Sammie Spencer.

"Sammie?" she asks.

"Yes, help us please," Sammie pleads.

"Can she walk?" Ashley asks, pointing to the girl in the bed.

"I don't think so," Sammie says, giving Ashley a desperate look that says she doesn't want to discuss how bad the girl's condition is in front of her. She just wants to get the hell out of there.

"Okay, I'm going to get you out of here and then I'll come back for her," Ashley promises.

Sammie doesn't hesitate before agreeing. Ashley knows she's desperate to get out of the bunker, but she's also surprised that Sammie doesn't have a stronger desire to save her fellow prisoner. She turns her flashlight off and climbs the stairs so hastily, she trips on them twice. She looks back to make sure Sammie is still behind her and as she nears ground level, everything goes black.

She awakens seconds later and is leaning forward onto the grass outside the trap door. Someone has hit her from behind, on the base of her skull. It hurts so badly she can't think of anything else. She looks around before spotting two sets of feet to her left. Her eyes slowly travel up to reveal her darling husband, Lincoln, and her only friend, Chelsey. Lincoln is shaking his head, and Chelsey is smiling with Ashley's duffle bag at her feet. She is fucking smiling. Did she tell Lincoln about Ashley's plan? Was she on his team all along?

Ashley spots a fallen branch within arm's reach and lunges for it. She has the sturdy wood in her hand and swings it in their direction so swiftly, she catches them both off guard, smacking them hard with the wood. She looks down at the hole beside her and sees Sammie's terrified face. Ashley takes advantage of Lincoln nursing his wound and strikes him again, this time across the face. She looks to Sammie desperately before knocking Chelsey to the ground and screams, "RUN."

Eighteen

SEPTEMBER 2023

RICH SUCCEEDS at most things in life because he is careful. He prepares. He overthinks every possible outcome before making a decision. Rich has kept the most-searched-for girl in America under his log cabin for twenty years without incident. Tonight, he realizes he's made the biggest mistake of his life. It's all because of Ronald. Fucking. Reagan.

He didn't even want to grant that little podcast pest an interview to begin with, but Nicole guilted him into it, and his mother told him she thought it would be a great way to keep the suspicion off the family. That interview could very well be the straw that breaks the camel's back.

He remembers the day in 2004 well. It was a beautiful summer day, and Rich still believed it was his own daughter he was protecting from Lincoln Palmer. He came downstairs to deliver her dinner when the nightly news came on the small TV he allowed her to have. He set the tray in front of her, transfixed by the breaking headline on the screen—Ronald Reagan has died at the age of ninety-three.

"Good," Malorie had muttered while she took a forkful of mashed potatoes and shoved them in her mouth.

"Good? Did you just say *good?* Ronald Reagan is *dead,* Malorie."

Rich was livid. He took the rest of her meal away and slammed the door behind him. Ronald Reagan was one of the last great conservative heroes, in Rich's opinion. How dare his own daughter disrespect his legacy?

This is the worst part of his mistake—he knew that Reagan died after Malorie arrived in his basement. He remembered it vividly. He slipped up and didn't even realize it until he came home and mentally replayed the entire interview. It was a quick anecdotal comment made in passing about what a bleeding-heart liberal Malorie was, and he didn't give it a second thought until it was too late.

Twenty years in, he's having to resort to an alternate plan to keep Malorie from being discovered and to save his own ass. He hastily unlocks the door to Malorie's room and throws a pillowcase on the mattress next to her. She's sitting on the corner, startled by his sudden arrival during a non-meal time.

"Put this on," he snarls.

She knows better than to ask any questions. Nineteen of her twenty years in captivity have been spent receiving little to no communication from Rich. She puts the pillowcase over her head and stands. He quickly ties a rope around her delicate wrists with a knot he learned as a child in Boy Scouts and never forgot. Silently, he leads her up the stairs and out to his truck, where he puts her in the back seat and tells her not to move.

Two minutes later, he's pulling down the gravel road to his vacant property when Lincoln Palmer passes him in his Cadillac Escalade. He has a female passenger that Rich doesn't recognize and he's driving too fast, even for his above-the-law, reckless ass. Rich shakes his head in disgust. It's bad enough that he treats this land like his own; the least he could do is not tear up his gravel drive by hot-rodding.

Rich checked the cameras—which Lincoln is still unaware of—last night and saw that the first bunker still appears to be empty. Lincoln hasn't been down there in months. Rich pulls as close as possible to the door of the bunker and shuts off his truck. He sits there for a moment, checking his surroundings before exiting the vehicle. He wants to be careful, but time is not on his side. He needs to get back to the house and clean up Malorie's room before anyone comes searching. It will be back to a doomsday prep room in mere hours, with any trace of Mal wiped away.

He grabs her shoulders, pulling the gaunt young woman upright before yanking her out of the truck and alongside him to the trap door. He hesitates for a moment when he sees that the leaves and debris over the door have been disturbed recently but doesn't have the luxury of time to investigate further. He swings the door open and pushes Malorie in front of him, mumbling for her to watch for the steps a little too late. She goes tumbling down, yelling in pain as she hits the ground with a thud.

"I told you to stay quiet," he barks.

She's crying now, but it's coming out in hushed whimpers as to not further upset the man who she's certain is finally going to kill her after all these years. He descends the stairs and cusses when he sees that the door to the bunker is wide open. He pulls his phone out of his back pocket and switches on the flashlight feature, scanning the empty bunker.

"That sloppy son of a bitch," Rich says. He's never seen Lincoln make a foolish mistake like this.

Rich doesn't even bother to remove the covering over her head as he pushes her in the room, throws a water bottle laced with sedatives in her direction, and locks the door behind him as he goes.

The sun is beginning to set as Rich pulls back into his cabin with a handful of cleaning supplies he retrieved from the Grab N Go. Luckily, the new employee behind the counter was too preoccupied flirting with Robbie, the deck hand from Benard's Resort, to notice Rich grab the spray bottles and rags from the back room.

As he's getting out of his truck to go home, his phone dings several times with an incoming call. It's one of his fishing buddies, Don. Normally he'd ignore the call, but Don spends the entirety of his retirement listening to the police scanner and is always the first to know when something is going down in Grady. If that good for nothing podcaster has called the sheriff, Don may be giving Rich a heads up about it.

"Hey Don, what's good?" Rich answers, attempting to sound as casual as possible while also in a hurry to get inside and clean up the evidence from the girl he's been keeping in his basement for twenty years.

"We got action," Don replies. It's always how he starts the conversation on busy scanner nights.

"Oh yeah?"

"They found the Spencer girl. The one who was missing from Benard's."

Oh, fuck. He knew Lincoln was messing too close to home with that one.

"Dead?" he asks. Why that son of a bitch can't get a lesson in disposing of bodies is beyond Rich. Rumor is they found the bones of a girl he killed years ago just this week, and they were very close to Rich's property line, which made him furious. This will be body number two. No doubt the FBI will be called in, so Rich is going to have to go back in the middle of the night and figure out somewhere else to bring Malorie. What a fine mess this is turning out to be.

"No, alive. She was wandering the old county road, completely filthy and dehydrated. Says she was being held somewhere underground this whole time. And guess who the fuck she says was keeping her hostage?" Don asks.

Rich grunts because speaking a single word may give away the fact that he knows exactly who was keeping her.

"Lincoln. Fucking. Palmer. Richie Rich himself. Sheriff says she made a positive identification. Fuck, Rich, Palmer lived here when that Benard girl went missing. You think he had something to do with that, too? This shit's crazy."

"You gotta be shittin' me," Rich replies, because he decided it's what he'd say if he was genuinely surprised by this news.

"I know," Don says, with zero hint of suspicion, thank God. "Alright, I'll let you get back to *Wheel of Fortune* or whatever you old people do this time of night."

"Alright," Rich says, his usual conversation ender. He presses the red button on his iPhone, slides it back into his jeans pocket, and mumbles "shit, shit, shit" repeatedly until he gets into the house.

He spends the next four hours scrubbing every inch of Malorie's room, careful not to use bleach because the smell will make him look guilty. He's watched enough television to know that. He brings down canned goods from upstairs to stack in the corners and throws random boxes from the other room in the basement to make it look like nobody has been inside his doomsday prep room for months. He leaves the door wide open as he sits on a pile of old throw pillows he has stacked on top of Malorie's mattress. Within minutes, the excitement of the day and the exhaustion from cleaning catches up to him and he dozes off, right there in Malorie's room.

By the time he's awakened by a strange noise, it's dark outside. He steals a glance at his watch to see it's the middle of the night. He hears the noise again. Someone is in the basement with him. He slowly rolls off the pillows and onto his knees, where he reaches to retrieve his Glock, still tucked in its holster on the edge of the mattress where he set it hours earlier. He stays as still as he can while he watches the black figure move around his basement. It's a man, small in stature, but big enough to put up a fight. He's digging through an open box of old pictures with a small flashlight. Rich sees the man pause when he comes across a polaroid and squints his eyes for a better look. He tucks it into his back pocket and turns, facing Rich directly. He gasps as Rich points the barrel of the gun directly at him . Within seconds of recognizing the figure as the same young man who interviewed him the day before, he pulls the trigger and shoots Nolan Cowell.

Nineteen

SEPTEMBER 2023

"WE'VE GOT the Spencer girl who was wandering on the north end of old country road, and we've got Fallon Palmer's body in the ditch two miles from the Grab N Go; but judging by the blood and dirt on the bottom of her feet, we think she traveled a while before collapsing. So we don't believe her attack scene is going to be too close," the local deputy explains to the Michigan State Police lieutenant, who just arrived on scene to aid in the search.

"And what has the girl mentioned about her surroundings?" asks the lieutenant.

"Not much, other than the fact that it was wooded. She's in pretty rough shape. Traumatized, understandably."

The lieutenant nods. "And where are we at on searching the Palmer property?"

"We've closed the resort, and all the guests have been evacuated. The search teams are still combing the grounds, but nothing has been found yet."

The lieutenant paces in front of the map of Grady,

which is laid out on the table before him. He's been to the lake a few times, but always for a weekend away to fish or hunt, so he never paid too much attention to the layout outside of the property he was renting and the bar he and his buddies would drink beers at when they were done. He's playing it cool in front of the young deputy, but this is by far the most exciting case he's been asked to participate in, and he's been on the force for nearly two decades. He vividly remembers the first time Grady was in the news because he was the same age as the young girl who went missing, Malorie Rose. He'll never forget overhearing his father tell his mother that night, "Thank god we didn't have daughters."

"From the limited information the Spencer girl has given the investigators, I don't think she walked far enough to have been kept on Palmer's Resort property," the lieutenant says, pointing at the X on the map before him. "If this is where the witness who called 911 found her on the road, she would have had to walk nearly two miles if she had been kept somewhere close to his resort. I don't think we're going to find anything there."

The young deputy nods in agreement and points to an area closer to where Sammie was found. "This land here belongs to Rich Lowery, owner of the Grab N Go. It's pretty centrally located between where Sammie turned up and where Fallon Palmer's remains were located. It might be a good place to focus on next. It's a few acres, and to the best of my knowledge, completely uninhabited. He's had a few very generous offers over the years but has refused to sell. Wants to keep it in the family."

The lieutenant raises his eyebrows, and it's the first time the deputy considers Rich Lowery being involved in anything at all immoral, let alone the kidnapping of a young girl.

"You don't think that—"

"Let's radio your superior and have him grab some men and meet us over there. I think it's worth a look."

Within an hour, an organized search has begun on Rich's land. Officers stopped at the Grab N Go when they couldn't get Lowery on the phone and got the approval from his mother, Mae Lowery, to begin the search. She said she hadn't heard from him all day, either.

As each officer is given a makeshift map with their assigned search quadrants, the young deputy receives a message over his radio from Sheriff Nelson.

"Hey Koski, you're over at Rich's land?"

"Yes, sir. Just beginning the search now, sir."

"Yeah, well, make it quick. I was just baiting my pile there last week, and I can assure you there were no missing girls wandering about."

"The Spencer girl says she was being held underground, sir. In some sort of bunker in the middle of a wooded lot."

Nelson's laugh catches the deputy off guard. "That sounds like every lot on this lake. Someone is going to need to get a better description from her or this is going to be a fool's errand. Let's not tie up all the department's resources until we have some solid information. Give the property a scan and then call it a night."

"Roger that, sir."

The visiting lieutenant is standing next to the deputy now, having heard the entire conversation. "These situations are always tough in a small town. I'm sure your sheriff just doesn't want his friend's property tore up. We'll make it as quick as we can."

Deputy Koski nods in agreement and decides not to share his annoyance over Nelson's request. They are trying to find where another girl may be dead or dying that was kept with Sammie in the bunker. He shouldn't care if it takes all night.

The dozen or so men and women begin their tasks, searching for any clues that a bunker door may exist beneath the heavily wooded land they are slowly venturing into, and for any evidence that may be left from the struggle that resulted in the death of Fallon Palmer. The first twenty minutes are silent, but for the crunching leaves and twigs snapping beneath their boots.

"We've got something!" a young officer yells. They've just crossed over into the second acre of the parcel.

Everyone else runs to join him and find a suspicious scene when they arrive. Several drops of blood litter the fallen leaves, and a bloodied tree branch lay snapped in half on the ground. A female deputy takes crime scene tape out of her bag and creates a barrier around the scene. Everyone else is frantically searching the area with their eyes, careful not to disturb anything that may look like evidence.

"Here it is!" a man yells, pointing frantically at a silver handle on the ground before him. "Permission to enter, sir?" he asks the visiting lieutenant, who is currently first in command on the scene.

After he nods his approval, the officers all draw their guns and get in formation to enter the bunker. They all exhale when he opens the entry door and a vacant stairwell appears. The officer in front motions for the others to follow him as he takes the steps one at a time until he's in the underground hallway, both his gun and flashlight trained on the steel door before him.

"Police! Put your hands up!" he shouts before pulling the handle. Much to everyone's surprise, the door is unlocked. They quickly survey the room and declare it free of any potential attackers before noticing a small lump under an old dirty blanket on a mattress in the corner.

"Hello? We're the police, we're here to help you."

The lump moves, revealing the gaunt, sickly face of a young woman. She blinks and raises her thin wrist, placing her palm over her eyes to shield them from the bright light coming from the officer. He quickly lowers it out of her eyes and radios the station to send paramedics. Sensing that the girl must be overwhelmed if she's feeling anything at all, he asks for his female colleague to stay and the rest of the officers to retreat and give them some room. Everyone complies.

Young deputy Koski and the visiting lieutenant begin walking away from the entry to the bunker to search for further evidence while they still have plenty of daylight to document it. They flag several footprints that are small enough to belong to either of the women and take a few photographs for good measure. Once they are nearly one hundred yards away from the bunker, the lieutenant sees something shiny from the corner of his eye. He can't believe it; it's another door handle, identical to the one they just discovered, leading them to a near-death girl who has been held against her will. His mind is racing with thoughts of what it could hold.

The man draws his gun and motions for the deputy to back him up, as he reaches down to open the door. They have a repeat of the view from the first door, simply a set of stairs and empty concrete hallway. He slowly climbs down and takes a deep breath before announcing himself. He then quickly pulls the door open, his heart nearly pounding out of his chest. These are drills they practiced at the academy and never anticipated they'd be put to use in the line of duty.

This bunker is also empty, but for one girl sitting upright on the mattress in the corner of the room. When she turns her head, he sees it's not a girl, but a woman.

Although she's aged significantly from the pictures used on the missing posters, news broadcasts, documentaries, and social media posts, he'd recognize her anywhere. It's the missing girl who has haunted this small town for twenty years. He drops his flashlight on the ground and falls to his knees in a rare moment of unprofessionalism. He can't contain his emotions.

"Malorie? Malorie Benard?"

The woman squints due to the light shining from the deputy's flashlight., He is now standing in the doorway of the bunker.

She quickly nods and begins to cry.

Finally, she thinks. *Finally, I'm going home.*

Part Three

Twenty

PRESENT DAY, HALLOWEEN 2023

BRENDA WALKS A CIRCLE AROUND US,
filling everyone's mugs with coffee because she's nervous and her default reaction is to be overwhelmingly hospitable in situations like this.

We're all here, in the family room of the lodge. Every seat in the room is filled, with Lou standing, leaned up against the door to the patio. Dougie and Nicole on the loveseat, Deb and Dad on the couch, Mal in the recliner that's normally reserved for Lou, but she'd insisted Mal sit there today. We've already told Dad the news this morning, and by we, I mean Malorie and me because she couldn't bear to do it alone. It's quite the one-two punch learning that your daughter had a stillborn baby while being held captive by one of your friends, who made her believe he was her biological father. Oh, and Mom didn't die of a heart attack on her peaceful winter walk back to Benard's from the Grab N Go. It's only 9:00 a.m., but I'm impressed the man isn't drowning himself in Jim Beam or at least adding a little to his coffee.

Malorie has asked me to give everyone the news at this family meeting, and although I'd rather be doing just about anything other than telling the two most emotional women I know that their sister's heart gave out after finding out her daughter was still alive, I agree to it because I'd do anything for Malorie. *Anything.*

The first wave of emotion strikes when I tell them about Mal being pregnant and the loss of the baby. Again, I honor Mal's wishes to leave Mae out of the story. Deb and Brenda gasp, Dougie stares at the ground, Nicole looks like she wants to murder her own father, and Lou and Dad are preparing for me to drop the bomb about the paternity.

"Malorie was only eighteen years old. She just found out she was pregnant, and she was terrified. I'm sure we all remember what it was like to be that young and the foolish decisions we made. Mal thought she was in love."

"With Rich?" Dougie asks and I want to slap him.

"No," Malorie jumps in. "Absolutely not. Rich never touched me. Not once."

I don't think anyone could anticipate the reaction Nicole has to that news. She drops to her knees and begins to cry so furiously; she's choking on her sobs. Deb and Brenda both rush to her side and kneel on the carpet.

"I'm sorry. I'm so sorry. What he did was horrible, Mal. It was horrible. I'm just so relieved to hear that. I've been thinking the worst. I'm so sorry," Nicole spits out, not making eye contact with my sister. Deb and Brenda are both rubbing her back, and she lets a few more tears flow before quickly wiping them away and apologizing to the room again for her reaction.

I rise from my seat on a kitchen barstool to join Mal. I perch myself on the armrest of her recliner and make eye contact with her before I begin. When we were young, I swear most of our communication was done without words. I'm hoping the magic still exists because I need her to know that I'm here. The rest of this conversation is going to get harder, but I'm here. We will get through this together. I cough lightly to regain everyone's attention.

"When Malorie was a senior in high school, she was groomed by Lincoln Palmer. He was the father of the child she lost."

Nobody can help flinching, but damn if they don't try. The focus shifts mostly to my father, who is now the front runner for candidates to murder Lincoln Palmer with his bare hands.

"Is there a statute of limitations on charging him for it?" Deb asks.

"There wasn't a crime committed, Deb. Mal was eighteen, and the relationship was consensual," Lou answers.

Malorie hangs her head in shame, and I want to shake her. She did nothing wrong. She thought she was in love. She thought he was going to leave his wife for her. She didn't know he was a monster.

"I know this is hard to hear, Nicole, but your dad told Mal that he buried the baby somewhere on his land. If you have any idea where we should start looking, speak up. We just want to give her a proper burial," Lou calmly speaks to Nicole.

"Her?" Dougie asks.

"I don't remember much from that day, but Rich later let it slip that the baby was a girl. When he realized she wasn't breathing, he said it would be best if I didn't see her, and I was in no position to fight. I didn't have any medication and kept passing out from the pain. I never told him, but I named her Gwen the day he told me she was a girl. I would love to put that on her headstone once we find where he buried her."

Gwen. After Gwen Stefani, Malorie's obsession as a teenager.

"I'm going to visit him in jail. Malorie, I'll do whatever I can to find out where she's buried," Nicole says in a somber tone. I cannot imagine what it's like to hear that your own father is capable of this level of cruelty.

"I'd appreciate that," Malorie answers quietly, avoiding eye contact with Nicole. She knows it's time to tell the family the rest of what happened. I grab her hand and ask if she'd like to continue or if she'd like me to do it. She squeezes my hand, takes a long inhale, and begins.

Malorie tells our family the entire heartbreaking story about Mom. She explains that for fourteen months, Rich believed he was Mal's father and had been plotting a way for them to become a family. She talks about the cold, snowy evening when Mom arrived in her room and she thought her nightmare was over, when in reality it was only just beginning. When she gets to the part about spending half the night with Mom's cold, lifeless body, she says, "Rich and Mae didn't come get her until almost sunrise."

"Mae? Rich and Mae? What do you mean Rich and Mae?" Nicole jumps to her feet. "What do you mean Rich and Mae?"

Mal's face is white.

"Malorie, did my grandma help my dad?"

With a single tear traveling down my sister's cheek, she nods.

Twenty-One

MALORIE HAS BEEN TOSSING and turning for
hours. I wouldn't have the heart to admit that it's keeping me
up, but each time I begin to drift off, I hear her rustling sheets.
When the bedside alarm clock reads 3:00 a.m., I cave in and
ask her if she wants to come lie with me, just like when we
were kids. Much to my surprise she agrees, and seconds later
she is waddling over to me, wrapped in Grandma's quilt.

For minutes, we say nothing. Both on our backs, staring at
the ceiling, which still contains a few scattered glow-in-the-
dark stars that used to fill our entire room until we got old
enough to stop thinking they were cool. I try to remember
how many years I longed for this exact scene. All the nights I
cried myself to sleep, staring at her empty bed, just begging for
one more night of us lying together and staring up at these
stupid stars that we begged Mom to buy us and bullied
Dougie into sticking on the ceiling for us. Now it's happening
and I just want to bottle it up and never, ever forget. We have a
lot of healing to do, but my sister is home. She is home, in my
bed, and nobody can ever take her away from me again.

"I used to lie awake in bed, begging anyone upstairs who

would listen, that I'd like to take your place. I pleaded for you to be brought home, even if it meant I'd have to go wherever you had been and do my time. I just loved you so much, I would have done anything, *anything*, to get you back home. I hope you know that," I tell her.

After a beat, she tells me, "I used to lie in my bed and rehearse what I'd say if Chucky from *Child's Play* snuck in here to kill me. I had an entire speech ready about why he should kill you instead of me because you were younger and had less friends."

"Mal, that's so fucked up. I was trying to have a nice senti-mental moment here."

With that, we explode with laughter, covering our mouths so we don't wake the rest of the family. I want this exact feeling every single moment for the rest of my life.

Seconds later, we hear footsteps coming down the hall. We've woken somebody up. There are two light taps on the door before it creeps open and Dad's face appears in the hallway light.

"Oh, shit," Mal whispers and this just makes us both laugh harder. "I didn't know you were sleeping at the lodge again."

"What the hell is going on in here?" Dad asks, and his genuine smile makes me want to leap out of bed and hug his neck. "I told you girls lights out hours ago," he says, and my heart aches at the memory of him telling us this as children when Mom would let him stay at the lodge during brief recon-ciliations.

"Dad," I whisper. "Mal used to plan out what she'd say to Chucky if he came to life so he'd kill me instead of her!"

"I know; I used to help her come up with reasons to help her cause," he replies without missing a beat.

Malorie throws her heads back and cackles. It's pure joy. Everyone in this country is chomping at the bit to see how Malorie Rose Benard is surviving, and I know this scene would bring everyone such comfort, but selfishly I'm happy it's just for us. I'll remember this night forever.

Dad walks over and sits on the edge of our bed.

"My girls," he says, reaching out a hand. Malorie and I each reach out to grab his and the three of us sit there for a moment before he speaks again. "You're my whole heart. I know tonight was very tough for the both of you, and I'm so proud of you girls."

We make small talk in hushed tones for a few more minutes before he leaves our room and Malorie waddles back over to her own bed. Within minutes, she's fast asleep and lightly snoring. It's the most beautiful sound.

Now it's me who is tossing and turning, finally giving up around 5:00 a.m. and tiptoeing out of bed. Lou is normally up by six, so I'll just start a pot of coffee and wait for her.

I'm surprised to smell one already brewing when I enter the kitchen. I don't see anyone in the family room, but the small porch light out on the balcony is turned on, so I pad closer to the window to see who is out there on this frigid morning.

Dad is leaned against the railing, bundled up in the same Packers coat he's been wearing since they won the Super Bowl in the nineties. I yank a thick blanket off the back of the couch, wrap it around my shoulders, and join him.

"What are you doing up so early, Katie Bug? Couldn't sleep?" I can see his breath coming out in little puffs in the near-freezing temperatures.

"I guess not. What about you?" I ask.

"Same, I guess. I'm just out here thinking about everything. All the mistakes in my life, all the things I wish I could do over."

"I thought you quit," I say, motioning to the lighter in his hand.

"I did. I guess I just carry this thing out of habit."

I hold out my hand and he drops the silver lighter into it, his initials engraved on the side.

"Dad, didn't Rich give this to you?"

He stares at the lighter, shaking his head.

"We were both so different back then. I never imagined the man he would end up becoming."

Twenty-Two

I HEAR Malorie moving around in our bathroom shortly after Lou wakes up. Moments later, she comes out of our room and pours herself a cup of coffee. Lou and I do our best to hide our surprised reactions. If Malorie is ever going to have a normal life again, we need to accept that there will be little victories like this every single day until she's back to good. Coming out of her room to pour herself a cup of coffee is a normal thing that normal people do, and we have to learn to better hide our reaction so she doesn't revert to the shell of a human she was just over a month ago.

Lou receives a text on her phone, seemingly responds to it, and sets it face down on the kitchen counter.

"Girls, I'd like you to hear it from me. I just got news that the other young girl they found in the bunker, Jordan Parker, has passed away at the hospital in Green Bay."

My heart breaks for her family. She had been missing for an entire year. They must have been overcome with joy and optimism when they heard she was found alive, only to be devastated a month later.

"Another life he took without remorse. What if our baby

had survived and she had to grow up with a monster for a father? I cannot imagine raising a child with Lincoln Palmer, knowing what I know now. I swear, in the weeks I spent with him, he didn't give any indication that this darkness lived inside him."

My mind briefly flips to an alternate universe where Rich never kidnapped Malorie. Where her baby girl survived, and she was forced to co-parent with that piece of shit. That baby would be in college now and I'm sure we'd still be dealing with the fallout of having Palmer DNA in this family.

Neither of us know what to say to that, so Lou pats Mal's back and I reach forward to squeeze her hand.

Dad left a few minutes before Malorie woke up, and he took the last of his things, so maybe he's really going to stay home full time now. He's been alternating between his place and ours since Mal got to the lodge. I'd like to believe he has enough self-awareness to realize that as life gets a little closer to normal again, so will the dynamic between him and my aunts. He is the drunk that broke their sister's heart and only performed half-ass attempts at fatherhood for most of our lives. The fact that they've allowed him to live under their roof and help at the restaurant is a miracle that only Malorie's homecoming could inspire.

"I also just wanted to mention that the next episode of Nolan's podcast drops today. The family and I gave our blessing before you came home . . . Now that you're back, I just want to make sure you're okay with Nolan airing some interviews that we gave him," I tell Malorie. Although Nolan will be crushed if Malorie is upset by the podcast, I know asking her is the right thing to do.

"That man put his life in danger and, as a result, I got to come home. I'd be willing to give him an interview myself if he wants," she says, and Lou and I are stunned.

"Mal, are you sure about that? Do you want to think on it a little longer first?" Lou asks.

Mal shrugs and takes a sip of her coffee. "It's the least I can do. It's not like it will be live, right?"

"No, no, he doesn't air anything live. He'd ask you a few questions, allow you to answer them differently if you feel like you've messed up, and he'll let you listen to it before it airs. Mal, this would change his life. I seriously can't thank you enough," I tell her.

"You really like this one, don't you Katie Bug?" Lou asks me, and heat instantly travels up my neck. I can't help but smile. I can't stand being smitten; it takes away all control over my emotional reactions. "Believe it or not, I think you could do a lot worse. He seems like a good kid."

That's the closest to a compliment that Lou has ever given someone I've been interested in.

"He lives in Chicago. I'm not sure we could even make it work," I sheepishly say.

"You'll never know if you don't try," Malorie tells me.

I still can't believe I'm standing in our kitchen, talking about boys with my sister. My *sister*.

"Well, I might call and tell him about the interview, if that's okay?" I ask Malorie.

"Remember when I used to make you call boys on speakerphone in front of me so I could analyze their tone and tell you if they were into you or not?" she asks, raising her eyebrow twice.

"Yeah, we're not doing that," I tell her with a wink and turn on my heels to shut myself in our room.

I peek my head back out and ask, "What day could you do the interview if he asks?"

She smiles. "My schedule is wide open at the moment."

I sit down on my bed and pull my phone off the charger. Lying on my back, I kick my socked feet up on the wall, just like I did as a teenager when I pinned the cordless phone from the kitchen between my ear and shoulder. Malorie is right; she used to force me to put whichever boy I was in love with that week on speakerphone so she could tell me her thoughts. Spoiler alert: her assessment was always that they didn't sound good enough to date her little sister. Annoying at the time, heartwarming now that I think back on it.

Nolan answers on the first ring.

"KB," he says, and I can hear the smile in his tone.

"I need a nickname for you. What do your friends call you?" I ask him.

"It used to be Cowell, but since the podcast blew up, it's usually 'bigshot,' 'asshole,' or 'Joe Rogan wannabe.' Take your pick."

I laugh. I'll stick to Nolan for now.

"I've got news for you," I tell him.

"Go on . . ."

"Malorie is going to do an interview," I say, giddily tapping my feet on the wall. Surely, it will wake Dougie, but I don't care. This is a huge deal.

"That's amazing, Katie. Who landed her? Oprah? *Good Morning America*? I'm sure they will treat her right. Just make sure you line up some ground rules before the interview."

"Nolan, with you. She's going to do an interview with you for the podcast. She said it's the least she can do for helping to bring her home."

For a moment, he doesn't say anything at all.

"Is this a joke?" he asks.

"I think you know me well enough to know I'd never joke about something this serious. She's doing exactly one interview, and it's going to be with you. Just let her know when."

I could be mistaken, but I think Nolan is fighting tears.

"Katie Benard, I don't know how I'll ever make this up to you. I don't think you understand what this means. It's going to change my life. I promise you I will only ask questions that I give to you and the family first, and she doesn't have to answer anything she doesn't feel comfortable with and—"

"*Nolan*!" I interrupt him. "Nolan, chill. We trust you. And you don't have to make this up to me. I didn't even ask her to do it. It was her idea."

"This is the best day of my life," he says without a touch of sarcasm.

"You must not have a very exciting life," I quip.

"It's ramped up since I met you."

"I'm off today. Want to grab lunch and talk about the interview questions?" I ask quickly before losing my nerve.

"I'd love to. Johnny's?" he asks, and it makes my heart flutter hearing that he's familiar enough with the local haunts to suggest one without hesitation.

"Johnny's is great. I'll meet you at my car at noon?"

"It's a date."

I'll never get sick of hearing him say that. I clutch the phone by my chest like a lovesick teenager once we hang up. Life is just so good again.

Twenty-Three

"KB," a voice shouts as I'm opening my driver's side door to verify that my passenger seat is clean for Nolan. I feel dizzy when I turn to see Bradford Palmer. Standing next to him is his mother, JoAnne, who I met at Benson's funeral.

"Bradford, JoAnne, good to see you both," I respond, not quite knowing what else to say. *How's life? Oh, your dad is in jail for kidnapping and murder, your stepmom and brother are both dead, and your family business is being seized? Fantastic!*

"We won't take up too much of your time," JoAnne begins. Despite the stress and public scrutiny, I'm sure she's been under for the last month, she looks very well put together. She has a look of old money, but from what I hear, she's worked for everything she has. She's fidgeting with the dainty chain around her neck, her hand wrapped around its charm. "Officer Nelson told us about the pregnancy, and he also told us that he somehow believes my ex-husband wasn't involved in Malorie's disappearance. I came here because I'm sure you understand how absolutely ludicrous that sounds to us. Lincoln held girls underground on that land for years, killed more than a handful that we know of, and the missing girl who was found in one of his bunkers magically had nothing to do with him, even though she was at one time pregnant with his child? It's just a little hard to wrap our minds around. Do you think she has reason to be covering for him? Does she understand the repercussions of lying about his involvement?"

I don't believe she intends to, but she's coming across as abrasive toward me, as if I'm somehow to blame for this mess. Bradford recognizes the tension and steps forward, between his mother and me.

"What my well-intentioned mother means to say is that we are so happy your sister is alive and well, and we were wondering if you could give us confirmation that my father really didn't have anything to do with her disappearance or captivity. We understand you have a lot going on in your life, but if you could just fill us in, we will be out of your hair immediately. Our SUV is packed up and we are ready to hit the road. I'm going to stay with my mom for a little while," he says, casually gesturing to the Toyota Highlander behind him, a few years newer than my own. It's strange to see a member of that family holding the keys to anything other than an unnecessarily expensive luxury brand.

"Bradford, I'm so sorry for everything you've been through in the last month. I can't imagine the pain and confusion. Yes, it appears that my sister had a relationship with your dad the summer after graduation, and yes, she was pregnant. That's the end of Lincoln's involvement in my sister's story, and I assure you she isn't lying to protect that man."

Sure, it's cold to refer to his father as *that man*, but it's a hell of a lot nicer than what everyone else is currently calling him.

"JoAnne, I have to ask you, how did you know Lincoln might be involved in Sammie's disappearance? I can't stop thinking about what you said to me at Benson's funeral," I ask the woman, and before the last words are out of my mouth, Bradford's head has snapped back in the direction of his mother. Wide-eyed, he waits for her response.

"Dear, you must have misunderstood me. That's not what I was insinuating. I was just as surprised as everyone else to learn that my ex had something to do with that poor girl's disappearance. I'm just relieved to hear he wasn't involved in Malorie's."

She's lying. I don't know why, but she's lying. I didn't misunderstand her. She whispered directly in my ear that I needed to find out if Sammie Spencer spent any time with Lincoln. Within a week, we found out he was her kidnapper.

"Yes, two kidnappers existing alongside each other in one of the smallest towns in Michigan. What are the odds, right?" I ask. Lincoln might not have been the one to take my sister, but something tells me he was very much aware of her location.

"We have to get on the road. We are very sorry to have bothered you. Please give your sister our best," the former Mrs. Palmer says in a curt tone before ushering a still-confused Bradford in the direction of their vehicle.

I'm watching them pull out of the Benard's parking lot when Nolan appears to my right, exiting the path that leads from the cabins to the lodge. He's not wearing a coat, only a thick sweater, and I have an overwhelming urge to make him turn around and add some layers. I haven't cared enough for someone to mother them in a very long time, and it fills me with a warmth in my chest I didn't realize was missing.

"Ms. Benard," he says as he approaches the car. "You're looking lovely this afternoon."

"Mr. Cowell, you don't look so bad yourself."

I quickly enter the SUV so he won't notice I'm blushing. What am I, a teenager?

"Dare I ask what the Palmers wanted?"

"Buckle up, it's a doozie."

On the way to Johnny's, I tell Nolan all about my conversation with JoAnne at the funeral. I can't believe I'm just telling him now, but both of our lives erupted in chaos shortly after that conversation with Lincoln's ex, so it's fallen down the priority list. I let him know about everything she asked me today and the irritated tone she seemed to have toward me.

"So, Nelson told them about the pregnancy? That surprises me. You may want to ask if she wants to discuss it on the podcast so she can get ahead of it hitting the news. If Nelson is already releasing the information, it's only a matter of time before the press gets ahold of it. They are already bribing locals for insider information."

I scoff. "They are trying to get Grady locals to talk? I'd love to be a fly on the wall for those conversations."

"Curtis Rivers was walking to the dock with his kid when some reporter stopped him and offered cash for info about Mal. I swear on my life, he took the cash out of his hands, burped, and kept walking. Once he had Brogan in the boat, he turned back and said 'and that's a direct quote' before speeding off. That man is my hero."

I cackle at the thought of someone trying to get a soundbite out of Curtis. I'll have to give him and his son both a milkshake on my next shift, his lactose intolerance be damned.

"I didn't know you'd met Curtis Rivers. He's a hoot."

"Katie, I've spent nearly two months sitting in a booth at Benard's. I think I've tried every item on the menu, and I've met every regular you have. I can tell you about Janice Evans's seven grandchildren in Minnesota, Gary Stewart's colonoscopy results, and the latest drama between your aunts. I'm basically a local," he boasts.

"Drama between the aunts? What now?" I say as I put the car in reverse.

"Lou is going to have to trust Dougie to manage shifts

pretty soon or Brenda is going to blow a gasket, and Deb is sick and tired of being caught in the middle of it," he tells me with feigned investment in the gossip. I can't help but smile. He really is fitting in like a local.

"Oh, boy. Let's get to Johnny's so you can fill me in on the rest of the town gossip over a large pepperoni pizza."

He shakes his head.

"Cathy Woodbury said they changed their crust recipe, and she is *not* happy about it. I told her I'd be the judge of that after I try a pie myself this week."

"Nolan Cowell, did you invite me specifically to Johnny's so you can report back to the town gossips about the quality of their pizza crust?"

He shrugs his shoulders and holds up his small notebook and pen, which are always with him.

"All I know is that I'll be giving Cathy and her friend Jules a full report when I get back to lunch."

"I adore you," I tell him with a smile, and from the bottom of my heart, I mean it.

Twenty-Four

"WHAT'S UP, NIC?" I ask when Nicole walks through the door with an expression glummer than the one she's been wearing all month. Something new has happened. I know her.

"I went to the jail to talk to Dad about the baby. I prepared my speech all day. I was going to appeal to his softer side so he'd talk to me about it. If he has a softer side left."

I raise both palms from my standing position in the kitchen. Truth be told, I was leaning on the counter texting Nolan, mildly annoyed when Nicole burst in the door and interrupted our flirtatious conversation, but now I see this must be important.

"Well . . . ?"

"Well, they told me I couldn't see him."

"Huh? They have to let you see him, don't they? Isn't there some sort of law that they have to get so many visits? I don't really know how this works, but surely there is."

I can't wrap my mind around how insane it is that I'm talking to my best friend about visiting her father, who is in jail awaiting trial for kidnapping my sister. What is this, *Days of our Lives*? Jesus.

"They said there was an *incident*, whatever that means," she tells me while kicking her shoes off and walking over to the pantry to grab a sparkling water, which she insists on drinking at room temperature. My stomach drops as my mind instantly goes to all the worst possibilities--someone has attacked Rich in his cell. Rich has gotten in a jail yard fight. Rich has taken his own life.

"Hey, Nic," Lou says as she comes in from her patio smoke break and hangs her Columbia jacket on the coat rack by the door, rubbing her hands together for warmth. She has been extra gentle with Nicole since Malorie let it slip that Mae was a participant in her captivity. After the initial shock, Nic seems to be handling it better than I expected. Or maybe she's just become numb to these bombshells by now.

I jump in and relay the news to Lou, because I know it exhausts Nicole to have to tell a story twice, particularly one like this.

"An incident?" Lou asks and I make eye contact with her behind Nicole's back, trying to relay how serious I think the situation might be. She nods.

"Yeah. I mean everyone else is in there for drunk driving or meth. It's not like a bunch of gang members are causing a yard riot. It isn't a prison, so I can't imagine what could have happened," Nicole says, hopping up on the counter instead of sitting on a barstool like a civilized human being. It drives Lou crazy, but she bites her tongue.

"I wouldn't worry too much about it, my dear. I'm sure they'll let you see him tomorrow."

Nic shrugs, grabs an apple out of one of the three fruit baskets on the counter and takes a bite. Fruit baskets, flowers, casseroles—we thought the gifts would stop now that Malorie has been home for a full month, but we were wrong. I swear something new gets delivered every day. The good news is, we haven't had to grocery shop for anything other than milk and eggs since September.

In true Nicole fashion, she sets the half-eaten apple on the counter and walks down the hall toward what has become her bedroom, my mom's old room. Lou and I stay silent until we hear her close the door and the thud produced when she falls onto the bed.

"What the hell do you think happened?" I whisper.

"That son of a bitch better not have taken the easy way out. I want to see him get sent to a real prison."

"You and me both," I say.

There is a loud knock at the door that nearly makes me drop the can of Diet Coke I just opened. I scrunch my nose and pick up my phone to check for security alerts—my smart watch usually vibrates when someone comes to the back door.

"Ah, hell kid, I had Dougie log into the app and turn off the notifications. They were driving me nuts," Lou tells me on her way to answer the door. Honestly, I'm surprised she lasted as long as she did with the alerts being sent to her phone and watch. She treats texts from her closest friends as an inconvenience, so getting notified every time a squirrel stops in front of our back door was bound to push her over the edge.

Lou peeks through the peephole and swings open the door to the lodge, revealing a tall, lanky police officer. He doesn't look familiar to me, but I've met a lot of officers in the last months so it's entirely possible we've met.

"Ladies, my name is Lieutenant Robert Barkley from the Michigan State Police. I've been in town working on the Palmer investigation. I was hoping to have a quick word with you both."

He's in his mid- to late-fifties, if I had to guess. Good looking man, if you're into that sort of thing. A quick glance at Lou confirms *she's* into that sort of thing. I'm not sure I've ever witnessed Lou Benard blush before this very moment. I stare at her for an extra beat because I want her to know I see it and that I'm enjoying this very much.

"Lieutenant Barkley, could I offer you something to drink? Perhaps a snack from one of our dozen gift baskets?" I say with a smile.

"Wow," he mouths, surveying the gifts on our counter, giving a low whistle. "I think I'm alright, but I might just grab one of those cookies on my way out." He gives Lou a subtle wink, and I think she might have a heat stroke. This is great. He's probably here to question us about mundane details like all the other investigators have this month, and I'll let Lou do most of the talking while I watch the show.

"Is Nicole Lowery still staying at your residence?" he asks.

"Yes sir, she is. Would you like us to have this conversation downstairs and out of earshot?" Lou inquires.

"No, actually, I was hoping she could join us."

Well, this is new. Nicole has been questioned separately a few times about her father, but never asked to participate in the inquiries regarding Palmer's case. I hear a door open down the hall. That nosy little gremlin must have been listening in. I turn toward her to see that it's not Nicole at all; it's Malorie. She just woke up from a nap. Robert Barkley looks like he's seen a ghost. He must be starstruck, like every officer other than Sheriff Nelson who has encountered Mal since her return.

"You," Mal says.

Lou and I both look in Barkley's direction. We've been present for all of Malorie's police interviews, and I think we'd remember if he had been in our house for an extended period of time before.

"It was you," she says and begins walking to the lieutenant. She gives us the shock of our lives when she wraps her arms around his waist and lays her head on his chest. He reluctantly hugs her back, a single tear traveling halfway down his cheek before he quickly reaches up to wipe it away.

"What in God's name is going on?" Lou asks. "How could you two know each other?"

"Aunt Lou, this is the officer who found me. He's the first face I saw. He saved me."

I now have the overwhelming urge to join in on the hug.

"I was just doing my job, ma'am," he says as he pulls away. His eyes are still glistening. I cannot imagine the shock he felt opening that bunker door and seeing Malorie. There's not a person in this state who doesn't know her face. "A local officer, Deputy Koski, was with me in the bunker that day. I'm sure he'd love to hear how well you're doing."

"Deputy Koski farted on my lunch in fifth grade and started a rumor that I was dating my cousin, Dougie; he doesn't deserve to know how my sister is doing," I respond. This gets a laugh out of everyone, which summons Nicole from her room because she can't stand for any of us to be laughing without her.

"What's so funny? Who are you?" she asks Barkley. No tact, ever.

"Nic, this is Lieutenant Barkley. He came to ask us a few questions; would you like to join us?" Lou asks her in the same tone she would use to make an uncomfortable request to a toddler. Nicole sees right through it.

"What's going on?" she asks, walking quickly to the table that we are all standing around.

"I'm actually not here to ask anyone questions," Barkley says. "I'm here with some news. Would you ladies mind having a seat? All of you."

Well, shit.

We quickly take our seats. Malorie doesn't know anything about "the incident" preventing Nicole from seeing her father today, so she's going into this conversation blind. Nicole doesn't seem to suspect the obvious conclusions Lou and I came to when we heard that she was denied access to her father today. We quickly meet each other's eyes before Barkley begins, and we prepare to comfort Nicole once again.

"Early this morning Lincoln Palmer was briefly transferred to Grady County Jail before a scheduled transport downstate to a higher security facility. Shortly after arriving at the jail, Palmer was attacked by several inmates. We have reason to believe that one or more employees of Grady County are responsible for putting Palmer in a position to be attacked. The officers we suspect were involved have been suspended, pending investigation. I'm here to let you know that Sheriff Nelson is among those involved."

"You think Nelson set Palmer up to get his ass kicked? Well, the man caused a lot of sleepless nights for the sheriff, so I can't say I'm surprised he let him get knocked around a little," Lou quips.

"He wasn't just knocked around a little, Ms. Benard, he succumbed to his injuries after being transported to the hospital in Marquette. Lincoln Palmer is dead."

"**WELL**, Sammie Spencer is willing to talk now that Palmer is dead. Apparently, she was convinced he was somehow going to escape and find her. She heard Malorie is giving me an interview so now she wants to be on the podcast, too. My head is spinning. I just scored the two interviews every journalist in this country is after."

Nolan finishes reading the email and sets his phone face down on the bar in front of him. I'm five hours into my shift, and it's the first time I've been able to stand still since I clocked in. Death in Grady Lake has proved to be even better for business than missing girls. Now that Benson Palmer's death has officially been ruled a homicide, that's two deaths in town within a month, both in the same family no less. Details have been scant about Jordan Parker, the teenager who never came out of her coma after being found in the bunker that held Sammie Spencer. From what I've heard, she didn't have much family and had run away from her foster home several times before she disappeared in 2022. So much for my vision of loving, grieving parents. Other than Sammie Spencer, most of the victims of Lincoln Palmer have come from similar backgrounds—underprivileged, uneducated, all but forgotten by their families. When I think of how the entire nation united in panic when Malorie disappeared, it breaks my heart to think that not all girls receive the same compassion.

As I'm refilling Nolan's drink, a woman I recognize but can't place walks into the restaurant and makes a beeline for me.

"You're Katie, right?" she asks.

"Yes," I say, holding out my hand. "You look so familiar, but I'm sorry, I can't place where I know you from."

"Oh, we've seen each other around. I worked at Palmer's Resort for years. My name is Chelsey."

That's it, Chelsey. I remember meeting her one drunken night at our local dive bar, The Moose Trap, when I was home for Christmas break. I redden slightly when remembering that I told her how good her hair smelled. We met that night; there is no earthly reason why I should have been close enough to smell her hair.

"I'm sorry to hear about the resort closing down. I'm sure the bank will find buyers soon; it's a beautiful property."

"Well, that's actually why I'm here. I know we're just heading into the off-season, but I was wondering if your family is hiring? I was head of housekeeping for Palmer's, but I think I've worked every position there in the last decade. I'd love to fill out an application."

This could not come at a better time. Most of Palmer's employees were seasonal and ready to return to their hometowns or home countries after summer ended, so we didn't get the influx of applicants we'd expected when the resort closed down. We are busier than ever and could really, really use the help.

"Hold on one second," I tell her and excitedly run to the

kitchen. Seconds later, I'm back with Lou in tow. None of us can hire anyone without Lou's approval.

"Lou, this is Chelsey. She worked at Palmer's for over a decade and—"

"You're hired," Lou says, shaking Chelsey's hand.

"Don't you want to know which positions I worked?" Chelsey asks, unable to hide the joy on her face from finding employment in the off-season, a rare feat in a non-ski town in northern Michigan.

"You're cute, you waited until after the lunch rush to apply, and you handled working for that jackass for over ten years? By my calculations, I think I'd hire you to work any position at this resort."

Chelsey flinches slightly at the word *jackass*, but quickly recovers with a smile. She's lived inside a bubble at Palmer's and probably isn't used to how the rest of the lake has viewed her ex-employer since the day he moved in.

"I will warn you," Lou continues, "during the off-season, we all pitch in where we're needed. Although, I think head of housekeeping would be a great title for you, and it's a role we need, but we may also need help in the restaurant or at the docks. Is that okay with you?"

"Yes ma'am, of course. I'm happy to help wherever you need me."

"How soon can you start?" I ask.

"Today," she says with a nod. "Just as soon as you need me."

"Fantastic," replies Lou. "If you can have a seat and give me fifteen minutes to finish some things up in the kitchen, I'll come out and do your new hire paperwork. Katie here will set you up with something to eat if you'd like."

"I've already had lunch, but I'd love a Diet Coke if that's okay," she says to me.

Ah, a girl after my own heart. I like her already. Which means Nicole is going to hate her. Her favorite mantra is *no new friends*.

Lou crosses paths with Dougie on her way back to the kitchen and quickly tells him about the new hire, nodding in our direction. I roll my eyes when Dougie slicks back his hair and begins to fidget. He makes a beeline for us. Oh, here we go.

"You must be Chelsey. My name is Douglas. I'm one of the proprietors here at Benard's."

Nolan spits his drink all over the screen of his laptop, hurriedly grabbing a stack of bar napkins to wipe it down. I last about half a second before I lose it, as well.

"Douglas, nice to meet you," Chelsey says, holding out her hand. "I actually used to room with Jackie Wilder." Her smile says it all. Jackie is one of Dougie's ex-girlfriends. The relationship ended when Dougie cheated on her with a girl from Marquette and was dumb enough to take her to a Packers game where they were shown together on the jumbotron, resulting in several of Jackie's friends, who were in attendance, texting her the news.

"Well, shit," Dougie says.

"Well, shit indeed," Chelsey replies with a wink.

Man, I like her. I hand Dougie the Diet Coke I just poured for her and ask him politely to show her to table twenty-one, Lou's preferred spot for completing onboarding paperwork with new employees. As he takes it from my hand and walks out from behind the bar to join her, I hear him ask her something about believing in second chances and, against all odds, she smiles. *Douglas* sure does know how to charm the ladies before they get to know him enough to be annoyed.

"That was amazing. I love small towns," declares Nolan.

"Maybe you should move to one," I say as a joke but quickly realize the implication. Although this flirtation has been going on for weeks, we have yet to acknowledge our feelings for one another. Well, I have yet to admit my feelings for him, and I can only hope and assume he feels the same way.

"All joking aside, the city has kind of been wearing on me lately. I think being in a town like Grady has been good for me."

"Could you see yourself . . . relocating to a small town?" I ask.

"My parents would certainly love it. They are worried sick about me living in Chicago. Every time there is a shooting on the news, they start calling me, convinced I was somehow involved."

"And where do they live?"

"Marinette, Wisconsin. It's a small town on the border. My stepdad took a job there after I graduated high school, and they fell in love with the community. It's right on the water; you'd love it," he tells me, and I smile. We have to drive through Marinette to get to Green Bay, so I know it very, very well.

"My mom used to take us to this restaurant there on our way to go school clothes shopping. It's called The Brothers Three, and they have the best pizza," I say, smiling at the memories. I haven't been to Wisconsin in years and wonder if it's still open.

"You're kidding. They take me there every time I'm in town. Which is nearly not often enough, according to my mother."

"Marinette is only two hours from Grady," I say and I'm not even sure what I'm suggesting.

"Katie, I like you. I really like you. A lot. I just want to make sure you know that. It's been driving me crazy keeping it inside."

I want to run circles around the lake, leaping in the air like they do in cheesy rom-coms.

"Well, that's a relief because I like you, too."

In fact, I'm not sure I've ever liked someone so much in my life. What a blessing that has come from a tragic, devastating series of events. The universe sure can throw some curve balls when we least expect them, right?

Twenty-Six

"YOU'VE sure been putting in overtime flirting with khaki pants," Nicole says as Nolan walks out the door and she clocks in for her shift.

"His name is Nolan, and he's wearing track pants today, Nicole."

"Because his arm is broken, and he can't button up his khakis, Katie."

"Because he has a bullet hole in his shoulder from your father, Nicole."

"Touché."

Dealing with Nicole's emotional highs and lows have been a struggle my entire life, but damn she makes me so happy when she's in this kind of mood. I guess dealing with her lows is just part of being her best friend, and although it isn't easy, it's the job I signed up for.

"Did they let you see Rich today?"

"Yeah. Yeah, they did."

"Want to talk about it?" I ask. She considers it for a moment before responding.

"Not really. He was a good father to me, but he's a

horrible man. I don't think it's healthy for me to continue to visit him. I've got some stuff I need to work through for my own mental health."

"Wow, Nicole. I'm really proud of you. Seriously."

"It's just weird having my entire family taken from me at once. Maybe I do need to talk to that therapist, if the offer still stands."

Just as the words come out of her mouth, Dougie is behind her and throws her into a headlock.

"We're your family now, you little bitch," he says as he rubs his knuckles on top of her head, ruining the perfectly smooth ponytail I know took her thirty minutes to master before coming to work.

"I didn't even like you when we were kids," she mumbles, walking to the bathroom to fix her hair.

"We need to keep an eye on her," Dougie tells me. "I know she's in one of her good moods today, but I have a feeling the down swings are going to be especially rough until she gets the help she needs."

"What's up with you two idiots both being insightful today? Is this the *Twilight Zone*?"

"Fuck off. Did Rich give her any idea where he buried the baby?" he asks.

"She didn't say, which means no. Maybe he's worried they'll charge him with murder if they have the body."

"Do you think he killed the baby?" Dougie asks.

"I mean, would you put it past him after all he's done?"

He's about to agree with me as we are interrupted by Chelsey, holding a stack of papers in one hand and the empty cup from her Diet Coke in the other.

"Lou said there were some menus she was going to send home with me to study. Any chance you know where they are?"

"I do," Dougie says. "They are in the office; I'll be right back."

Chelsey takes a seat at the bar as Dougie wanders off to grab her study materials. Moments later, Lou appears by my side, and the stench of smoke means she's just taken a break. She leans forward to wash her hands in the bar sink and says to me, "I caught up with Nolan outside as he was leaving. He said Sammie Spencer is coming back to town to give an interview?"

"Yeah, that's what I hear. She said if Malorie trusts him, so does she. She's reportedly turning down offers for some pretty big paydays from the TV networks to do his podcast for free. It doesn't make much sense, so I guess we'll see if she actually shows up this weekend."

"It would be nice if she gave a description of this second kidnapper so we know if it was a local or not."

This whole damn time, the public has assumed her comments about a second kidnapper were referring to Rich Lowery. Very few people know that she told investigators he doesn't fit the description of the second man who took her.

"He took girls from at least three different states and had business dealings all over the country. There's no way the other guy is local if it's not Rich. I'm sure it's some other wealthy asshole who traveled here to join in on his fucked-up crime spree."

"So, you think she'll talk about the other kidnapper on the podcast?" Chelsey asks, catching us both off guard. "Sorry, didn't mean to butt in, but I couldn't help overhearing. I think we're all a little obsessed with the story, especially those of us who thought we knew Lincoln Palmer."

"For everyone's sake, I hope she does." I say. "It would give us a better idea of who we are looking for, and it would be rating's gold for Nolan. He deserves a big payday after all that he's done for us."

"Can't argue with that," she says.

Dougie arrives back with the menus and an info sheet detailing the history of Benard's Lakeside Inn, which Lou likes every employee to know because tourists often inquire about it.

"Anything else you need Chelsey to do before she goes, Lou?" he asks.

"Get some rest, we're planning on being slammed tomorrow on your first day. We're really happy you're joining the team," Lou tells Chelsey with a rare smile, which looks like it's physically paining her to wear.

"I'm really happy to be here and can't thank you enough for the opportunity."

"Here's my number in case you have any questions," Dougie says, handing her one of the business cards he inexplicably had made at the local printer last winter.

She doesn't look at it, simply takes it and tucks the card in her back pocket.

"Thanks *Douglas*, but I don't think I'll be needing anything."

She turns to leave, and as the door closes behind her, Lou nods and says, "I think I'm going to like that girl."

Twenty-Seven

"WHY ARE YOU SO NERVOUS?" Mal asks Nolan, and he can't hide his embarrassment. He's been building an impressive following for his podcast since he launched it five years ago, but being the sole person to land an interview with Malorie Rose Benard is sending him into the stratosphere. His podcast partner, Karli, flew into Marquette this morning to help with the interview, but she seems just as flustered as Nolan. It's kind of sweet.

"I'm sorry, we're almost set up here. It won't be much longer," Nolan replies, fumbling with the audio equipment. We're in the Benard's cabin he's been renting for weeks. The lodge and restaurant were too noisy, and the advantageous old-timer who runs the only radio station in town wanted a "cut" of the profits for allowing Nolan to use his garage studio, so he politely declined.

Here we are, huddled in the corner of the cabin at the small breakfast table with thick blankets hung all around us. Malorie doesn't seem nervous at all, despite being moments away from her first and only media interview. She's had a sort of calm wash over her in the last few days. I asked her about it when we were going to bed last night, and she told me she is finally starting to believe that she's home for good and nobody is going to take it away from her. It breaks my heart to think she ever believed otherwise.

"Lucky for you, Nolan, I don't have any plans, and I'm happy to finally be out of the lodge for a few hours."

Other than a few doctor's appointments in Marquette to assess her ongoing health issues due to her years with lack of sunlight and proper nutrition, Mal hasn't left the lodge at all. A few high school friends have contacted me to see her, but she says she's not quite ready for that yet. I can't imagine what it will be like to reunite with the friends that got to live the life she missed. College. Boys. Careers. Kids. I'm not sure I'd be strong enough to ever face it.

"I'm sorry if it's irritating to hear this over and over, but I followed your case my entire adult life. I used to lie awake at night, praying you were okay. I am just so happy to see you alive and well," Karli tells my sister, with a hint of hesitation.

"It's not irritating at all. I can't thank you enough for the prayers. I know a lot of people thought I was never coming home."

"I was this close to pushing your bed against mine and buying a king-sized comforter," I tell her. "One more week and I was going to toss your CoverGirl makeup from 2002."

Mal smiles and squeezes my hand. I've been trying to joke with her a little more, as she admitted that it makes her feel at ease and maybe even a little normal. Everyone has been walking on eggshells around her since she got home, and she just wants to feel like part of the family again.

"Okay, I think we're ready," Nolan announces, handing Mal and I each a set of oversized headphones.

For the next two hours, the four of us carry on a conversation that flows so well you'd think it was rehearsed. There are moments of laughter, of terror, of tears. I just want to squeeze

Malorie for handling this so well. The entire family is going to be incredibly proud of her. The entire nation will want to hear this podcast. Nolan and Karli do an amazing job of asking the tough questions but phrasing them in a way that is not offensive or invasive. They are complete professionals. When we are done, we all remove our headphones and Malorie begins to cry.

"I'm so sorry, I'm not even sure why I'm crying. That just felt so good. It was like an intense therapy session with friends. I can see why my sister likes you so much," Mal says, that last sentence directed toward Nolan.

He and I both react awkwardly as Karli watches in amusement.

"Okay, off the record, what *is* going on with you two?" she asks.

"Well, we . . . " he begins before gesturing for me to continue.

"We just, ahh . . . " I don't quite know how to answer the question. "Well, I like Nolan. A lot."

"I see that," Karli says, her smile so intense it makes me smile in return. "For what it's worth, I think this is great. I've been working alongside Nolan for five years, and I've never seen him show interest in much of anything that isn't work-related. This is refreshing."

"I think it's great, too" Malorie adds, raising her eyebrows and giving me a look that only big sisters can. God, I'm so happy to have her back.

"Okay, okay, that's enough," I say. "What time is Sammie coming?"

Nolan checks his watch. "She's flying into Marquette with her mother at four. Karli and I are going to buy her dinner and do a little interview prep, and then we'll record first thing tomorrow morning."

"I can't believe they are coming back to Grady," I say.

"You and me both. We have Malorie to thank for this," he says, gesturing toward her.

"I'm just trying to get you those advertising dollars so you can buy my little sister something really nice," she says with a smirk. She sure fell right back into being a major pest in my life after a twenty-year hiatus.

"Alright, Mal. Time to go. Thank you both for handling her first interview so well. We appreciate it more than you know," I tell Nolan and Karli as Mal and I stand to leave.

"First interview? This is going to be my only interview. I have no desire to talk about this again until I'm forced to do it in court," Malorie says as she pulls on her jacket.

Nolan and Karli steal a quick moment of eye contact, and I know what they are thinking—Malorie's *only* interview? This is going to go down in history. I know we all still think about Jaycee Dugard's *People* magazine interview. It was the first time any of us got to hear her version of events during her eighteen years in captivity, and we hung on every word. I don't even want to get into the foolish hope it gave me that Malorie would one day be found alive. I guess it's not so foolish now.

"We can't thank you enough, Malorie. You too, Katie. We will send you both a link to the episode before it goes live so we can take out anything you're not comfortable with. Katie, I've got your email, but I don't believe I have yours," Karli says, looking at Malorie.

"Well, the last time I had access to an email address it was in 2003, and I believe it was hottie1234@hotmail.com. Not sure I remember the password, so maybe just email the file to Katie and we'll listen together."

I can see the relief in Karli's eyes that Malorie has a sense of humor about her faux pas. She's been locked underground for two decades, Karli, c'mon. What's next, asking her if she has Facebook? I do wonder if Mal will ever hop on the social media bandwagon. If I had to guess, I'd say absolutely not.

As we open the door to the cabin, I peer out to make sure there aren't any photographers or lurkers before allowing Malorie to come out. Luckily, it's just chilly enough for everyone to be inside.

"Want to go for a drive?" Mal asks me, and I'm not sure what to say. I'm not sure what I'm *supposed* to say. She sees me stalling and laughs. "Want to text Lou and tell her we're going for a drive, so she doesn't freak out?"

"Now you're talking," I smile. Sure, Malorie and I are in our late thirties, but given the circumstances, I like the idea of looping Lou in on our plans. I shoot our aunt a quick text, and she is surprisingly on board with the idea, saying a nice fall drive sounds lovely.

"Where do you want to go?" I ask her.

"Anywhere but here."

I smile, knowing just the place.

She seems mildly nervous in my passenger seat, but I suppose it's been a long time since she's rode in a moving vehicle. I drive as carefully as I can but tense slightly as it begins to snow. The first snow of the season. I'm damn near being an expert at winter weather driving by now, but I worry she's going to be uncomfortable with the conditions. I steal a glance at my sister, and she has tears in her eyes.

"Is it my driving? Do you want to go back?" I ask.

"It's beautiful," she responds, looking out the window. "I forgot how beautiful it is."

I remember the doctor telling us that Malorie got little to no natural light exposure during captivity. Is it possible she didn't get to see freshly fallen snow at all while she was held against her will? The more we learn, the more surprised I am that my dad hasn't broken into the jail and killed Rich with his bare hands.

We drive for the next thirty minutes in silence and she doesn't ask once where we are going, which is great because I want to surprise her. When I take a turn at the green sign that says Kitch-iti-Kipi, she claps her hands together.

"Katie Bug, I haven't been here since we were in elementary school!"

"I haven't been here in years, either. It's a weekday and it's snowing, so I'm hoping the odds will be in our favor that there aren't many tourists here."

My heart soars when I see one other car in the parking lot. Kitch-iti-Kipi is the biggest natural freshwater spring in Michigan. It's just one of those places that can't be described in words, you have to see it for yourself. The water stays at forty-five degrees year-round and is crystal clear. The state park features a small raft on a pulley system that travels over the spring, the glass bottom allowing for a view of the water below you, including a healthy supply of trout that live in the lake. There is no swimming, fishing, or boating allowed. The Ojibwe appropriately nicknamed the spring "Mirror of Heaven."

We check in at the main building before taking the short hike down to the spring. A ridiculously friendly older woman is working the counter and offers us hot chocolate when she notices we are shivering from the outside temps. Zero recognition registers in her face as she politely smiles while I pay for our drinks. We are just two anonymous tourists, checking out this beautiful state park. Nobody needs to see my ID and gasp at the last name. We both needed an afternoon of blending in.

Mal and I make small talk on the path to the raft's entrance, sipping our hot chocolate and pulling our hoods up to deflect the increasingly thick snowflakes. Each year we seem to get one good snow in November, but it will be melted by tomorrow with forecasted temperatures in the forties for the rest of the week.

Just as I'd hoped, the raft is empty. We have the entire spring to ourselves. I pull my phone out of my bag to snap a few quick pictures to show Nolan later. I don't care how much of the world you've seen; this view is breathtaking.

The body of water over which the raft floats is only two hundred feet across and forty feet deep. It's surrounded by lush pine trees with tips that are now snow covered and resemble those fancy flocked Christmas trees you see in nicer homes each December. The water is nearly turquoise in color and completely translucent. The sight of twigs, logs, and passing fish is like looking through the walls of an aquarium.

"We are so lucky," Mal says before looking to the sky and allowing the snow to briefly accumulate on her eyelashes before she giggles and wipes them off. I cannot fathom the percentage of people who live through an event even half as tragic as what Malorie has experienced and use it as an excuse to never enjoy another minute or appreciate their surroundings. I'm not sure if it's Dalia's doing, or if my sister is just this strong mentally, but she sure is coming around at a healthy pace.

"Yes, we are," I respond, holding out my hand to gesture for her to walk onto the raft first. If I had to guess, it's built for twenty to twenty-five people, so it feels enormous with just the two of us. The entire center is glass-bottomed, and there's a large wheel to turn which pulls the raft across the lake and back. I pull a pair of gloves out of my pocket and man the wheel so Malorie can enjoy the view. She leans over and looks down through the glass the entire way, gasping each time she sees a school of fish or rapidly moving group of minnows. I wonder how long we could just go back and forth across this pond until somebody makes us stop. I don't ever want this to end.

"Katie, I'm going to be okay. I want you to know that. And I love you so much for having patience with me while I heal," she tells me as we depart the raft, safely back on shore. The snowfall is slowing, but the white blanket it has laid over the walking path has brought a magical silence to the woods. Our conversation and crunching footsteps are all I hear.

"Mal, I'll have patience with you until the end of time. I just can't believe you're home. I hope you know I'm here whenever you want to talk about things. I guess I just assumed I should leave the hard stuff to the professional."

"Yeah, I think Dalia is probably better equipped to handle the hard stuff," she says, reaching over to squeeze my hand.

She's already told us about the loss of her baby and the circumstances around the death of our mother; I can't imagine what could be harder than that.

"Well, I'm here for the hard stuff when you're ready and the fun stuff in the meantime," I tell her.

"I haven't had fun in twenty years; I'm ready to make up for lost time," she says with a mischievous look.

"Oh boy," I respond, not quite sure I have the energy for that kind of fun anymore.

"Remember that time we hid blueberries in Lou's work shoes and she blamed Dougie?" she asks.

I had forgotten all about that summer. She put Dougie on dish and dock duty for a month, ignoring his insistent pleas that he wasn't guilty. The thought of having an entire summer of good old-fashioned pranks with my older sister feels too good to be true. This much is certain—I'm never taking another second spent with her for granted, ever again. My sister is home, and nothing could be better than that. It's a constant struggle to control my boiling anger and frustration for the man who took so much precious time from us.

Twenty-Eight

AFTER NOLAN'S dinner with Sammie and her mother, he takes a break from interview prep to join me for a drink at The Moose Trap. I'd love to have him over to watch a movie, but with a lodge full of relatives and a bedroom I no longer have to myself, there's not much room for privacy. I'm a thirty-five-year-old who has nowhere to go with a boy. I'd be ashamed if I weren't so damn happy to be home with Malorie.

Normally I'd walk to the bar from Benard's, but the weather is a little too cold for that tonight so Nolan drives. It's only a half mile down the road, so surely my motion sickness can handle the journey. I've never been in his car before, but it's exactly how I pictured it—empty coffee cups, Post-it notes with podcast ideas stuck everywhere, and a few crumpled up McDonald's bags. I must have it bad because I find the mess to be charming.

He hurriedly swats a few things off the passenger seat and apologizes three times before I stop him.

"Nolan, you're a man. This is what men's cars look like, especially one who works as much as you. We're going less than a mile to go grab a few beers. I promise you it will be okay."

He exhales and seems to accept it. I buckle my seatbelt while he reaches over and squeezes my knee once before putting the car in reverse. It was an absent-minded gesture, I'm sure, but it gives me butterflies.

The flakes have grown since this afternoon and look like floating cotton balls under the parking lot lights when we pull into the bar. There's nothing like having a drink at a northern dive bar in weather like this. We exit the car and quickly scuttle toward the entrance, Nolan wrapping his arm around me in a chivalrous gesture to keep me warm.

The bartender, a guy named Jay, whom I've known my whole life, greets us as we make our way to a tall bar table and hang our wet coats on the back of two empty barstools. He lets us know there's a pot of chili and some bowls in the corner with packets of crackers on the end of the bar.

"I'll buy you a cup of chili, but I'm still stuffed from dinner. I had Lou's meatloaf special at Benard's," Nolan tells me.

"There is no buying a cup of chili, my friend. It's free."

"I don't understand," says Nolan, who has lived in Chicago all his life.

"Sometimes bars do this on cold days, especially the ones that don't serve food on the menu. During the summer, one of the owners makes a smoked whitefish dip that's to die for."

Nolan looks at the chili and then back at me. It's like this is a foreign country to him.

"I love it here," he says for the dozenth time.

We both look over the cocktail menu and decide that this is perfect hot toddy weather. I happen to know Jay makes a fantastic one because I used to order them when I was home from college on Christmas break. He mouths "hubba, hubba" and makes an immature lewd gesture behind Nolan's back as he walks away from the bar, both drinks in hand. I roll my eyes.

"So, how did it go with Sammie?" I ask, blowing on the top of my still-too-hot hot toddy.

"Better than expected. She bonded really well with Karli, and with her mother's permission, I have a feeling she's going to drop some bombshells tomorrow morning during the interview. She kept starting to open up, and her mother repeatedly reminded her that we were at a restaurant and the conversation would be better had tomorrow morning. It was interesting."

"Well, now you've got my attention. What do you think she's going to say about the second kidnapper?"

"I'm not sure, but her mom corrected me when I referred to the suspect as *he*. She held her hand up and said, '*he* or *she*,' the person was wearing a mask, and Sammie only assumed it was a male in her panicked state."

Wow. A woman? The thought never crossed my mind. I've been giving every male stranger in this town the side eye all month. Sammie is pretty fit; I'm surprised a woman could overpower her.

"So, do you honestly think a woman was involved, or is Sammie trying to protect someone?" I ask.

"I really don't know. There's so much more I'm dying to ask her. I don't think I'll sleep at all tonight."

He's adorable. He really does love his job.

"Also, Karli and I got a lot done on the interview with you and Mal. It is sounding really, really good."

"What are you going to call the episode? *The Sisters Benard*?"

He pauses to consider it before I tell him I'm joking.

"I was thinking just Season 5, Episode 4, 'Sisters Reunited,'" he tells me.

"Right to the point; I like it." I smile. "Oh, I wanted to show you a few pictures I took today when Mal and I went for a drive," I say, pulling out my phone. I open to the first picture taken at Kitch-iti-Kipi and hand him the phone. Silently, he flips through the pictures, slowly shaking his head.

"KB, this is the most beautiful place I've ever seen. Where is this?"

I tell him all about the water, the park, the history. He hangs on my every word.

"This area really is something else. I wish more people knew about the Upper Peninsula."

"I don't," I tell him with a wry smile. "We have enough tourists."

In the next hour, we order a second round of drinks, talk in depth about his family and my college years, and as the liquor settles in, I mentally beg for him to kiss me. He doesn't seem to receive the message and cluelessly continues to make small talk. Before long, I glance at the clock behind the bar and see that it's nearly ten.

"As much as I don't want this night to end, Lou has me on kitchen prep first thing tomorrow morning because Deb has to go get her driver's license renewed or something. If I don't go to bed soon, I'm going to be a zombie tomorrow."

I reach for my purse, and he holds up his hand.

"Are you nuts, Katie Benard? I've got this."

I shrug. It's been a while since a man scoffed at me when I reached for my purse. Even with Dave's salary eventually outpacing my own, he didn't say a word when I continued to pay for dinner.

I gather my belongings and put on my still-damp coat while Nolan goes to the bar to pay. I see him give Jay an odd look before throwing a few bills on the counter and thanking him.

"What was that about?" I ask as I zip up my coat.

"I think he might have given us a friends and family

discount or something. I reminded him that we had four drinks total, and he insisted that it was only twenty dollars."

Every time he acts like an out of towner, I like him a little more. This is funny because clueless tourists usually get on my damn nerves.

"Oh, sweet Nolan. That's just what drinks cost here," I tell him, looping my arm through his. We say goodbye to Jay on our way out and, although it has stopped snowing, the parking lot looks like a Thomas Kinkade painting when we push the heavy wooden door open.

He walks me to the car and before opening the door, he leans forward and finally gives me a soft, gentle, perfect first kiss. He smiles as our lips part.

"Sorry I waited all night to do that, but I didn't want our first kiss to be inside a place called The Moose Trap."

"Well, I'm happy to tell our grandkids that our first kiss actually occurred *outside* of a place called The Moose Trap."

And with that, he kisses me again.

Twenty-Nine

MY ALARM CLOCK physically hurts when it begins to beep. Even Malorie groans for me to shut it off. I remember that I'm scheduled to do prep work in the kitchen, and I groan as well. The memories of last night with Nolan float to the surface and the dread instantly leaves my body. My sister is home, Rich is in jail, Lincoln Palmer is dead, and I'm in love.

"The sun isn't even up yet," Malorie mumbles and pulls the covers up over her eyes.

"Some of us have to work for a living; we don't just get to kick it all day," I say mid-stretch. "Too soon?"

"I'd get kidnapped all over if it means I never have to wake up this early again in my life."

Hah! That's the sister I know and love. *She's back.*

I know it's going to be a good day because when I shut myself in the bathroom and glance in the mirror, I don't have a single blemish on my face. I don't think I've had a day since puberty without at least a small spot of acne. I comb my hair up into a messy bun, and it actually looks stylish instead of my normal resemblance to Miss Trunchbull from *Matilda*. I find that I remembered to wash, dry, *and* hang up my uniform after my last kitchen shift, and when I tiptoe out of the room and into the kitchen of the lodge, someone has just brewed a fresh pot of Michigan Cherry coffee.

The light on the balcony isn't turned on, but I know Lou is out there because I can see the small red dot burning at the end of her cigarette.

"Hey kiddo, glad to see you up. We've got a big weekend to prep for," she greets me as she comes back inside.

"Well damn, Lou. I've already got my coffee and I'm ready to go to work. Quit messing around and let's go."

This gets a genuine smile from her. Is there a better feeling than getting cranky Lou to crack a smile? I'm batting a hundred on this beautiful morning.

She tells me to go on without her and get the place unlocked while she 'goes to see a man about a horse,' which means she needs to use the bathroom and wants privacy.

Although there's a chill in the air, it's nowhere near as cold as it's been. I can actually breathe without the frigid air burning my nose. When I near the restaurant, I see that someone is crazy enough to be loading supplies onto their fishing boat. You've got to *really* love fishing to get up this early and out on the lake this time of year. I walk past the restaurant and closer to the dock so I can see if it's a local. Sure enough, it's Curtis Rivers and his son, Brogan.

"You've got that little angel out here before the sun is up?" I joke.

"I'm the walleye master, Miss Katie. I'm going to catch the biggest fish you've ever seen!" Brogan says, clapping and stomping enough to rock the boat.

"Well, you better come see me for a milkshake when you're done."

This gets a cheer from Brogan and a cuss word muttered by Curtis, which was my intention. I wave to them both and walk back to the rear door of the restaurant to unlock it for the other employees who will be in shortly. It's still dark enough to need the flashlight on my phone to find the correct key on Lou's massive ring of unmarked keys. As I'm searching, I hear the crunching of fast-approaching footsteps on the gravel. I place the keys between my fingers and hold them up as a weapon, which I learned in a self-defense class my former job in Lansing made all the women take.

"Hah!" I yell as loudly as I can, hoping to catch the attacker by surprise.

When I spin to confront him, I see an extremely pleased Nolan holding a box of donuts.

"That's it? That's the attack noise?" he says, barely containing his amusement.

"I knew it was you," I lie before cracking a smile. "What in the world are you doing up this early?"

"I couldn't sleep, so I figured I'd make sure your morning was off to a good start," he answers sheepishly. He hands over the box of donuts and tells me they are for me to share with the opening crew.

"How generous of you to assume I won't eat the whole dozen," I tell him, opening up the box. "Apple cider cake donuts? Maple glazed? Strawberry with sprinkles? These are all my favorites!"

"I know men aren't historically great listeners, but hosting a podcast has really strengthened my skills. I remember you mentioning the donuts when we first met."

"You are my hero. There's no doubt my morning is going to be great now. And yours will be, too. You're going to nail this interview; I just know it."

We sneak a quick kiss just before the first line cook pulls into the parking lot. Nolan shines my flashlight on the keyring I'm holding until I get the back door unlocked, and then he hands the phone back to me, his hand wrapped around mine for a few seconds longer than it needs to be.

"Break a leg," I tell him. "Or whatever the podcast equivalent is."

"Are those donuts?" Paul says as he passes between us and grabs the box out of my hands. I guess that's my cue to get to work. Nolan quickly kisses the top of my head and disappears onto the half-lit path to his cabin. I don't wake to see the sunrise nearly often enough. This time of morning is so beautiful. Am I so smitten with this man that I'm becoming a morning person? It's ridiculous.

Lou's drill sergeant instructions don't bother me a bit for the next five hours while we chop, dice, marinate, portion, and label. Whatever kind of business this weekend brings, we'll be ready for it. Dougie's juvenile insults aimed at me each time he comes back to the kitchen to refill his ice bucket actually make me chuckle a few times. When Deb gets back from her "administrative errands," she offers to clock in and relieve me, and I tell her to take the rest of the day off. I'm in a groove and somehow don't mind the work at all.

The cooks are playing Yacht Rock Radio, which is my very favorite, and we're all humming along to the songs. When I prep some extra bar fruit for Dougie, I pop up front to deliver the containers and see Jenna and Hoda on the *Today* show talking about Thanksgiving recipes. I can't believe it's close enough to the holidays to be talking about recipes.

"Shouldn't these TVs be on football?" I ask Dougie.

"It's Friday morning, dumbass," he replies, and I laugh. I wholeheartedly laugh.

"What the hell is going on with you, anyway? You've been somewhat pleasant to be around. I don't like it. It's suspicious."

"Oh, Douglas. Can't I just be happy?" I say, spinning on my tiptoes before returning to the kitchen.

After the lunch rush, Nolan comes in to sit at the bar, and

after making him a drink, Dougie comes back to the kitchen to let me know.

"Go ahead, take the rest of the day off, kid. You worked like a real Benard today," Lou tells me, which is the greatest compliment that can be given in this establishment. I stick my tongue out at Dougie because he'd kill for Lou to tell him the same.

I take my filthy apron off and throw it into the bin for the weekly linen pickup and peek my head into the employee bathroom briefly to check my appearance before going up front. My luck continues when I see that I don't look half bad, and the flushed cheeks I have from working in the hot kitchen somehow suit me.

Dougie is leaned forward on the bar talking to Nolan when I emerge from the kitchen, and he spins to greet me with a smug look on his face.

"What's your deal?" I ask him.

"Your man friend here just told me that Chelsey did a fantastic job waiting on him last night for dinner and that she's a real asset to our team. Looks like someone did a great job training her and that someone is me."

I scoff.

"You let Chelsey take tables on her own, Dougie? She hasn't even passed the menu tests. You need to think with your head instead of your other body parts for once."

"Whoa, I didn't mean to get anyone in trouble. I was just trying to pay you guys a compliment. I know you're always looking for good employees, and it seems like you found one," Nolan says, his palms up in defense.

"No, you did nothing wrong. It's just that we have a pretty stringent training policy around here, and my dear cousin likes to let females skip a few steps when he finds them attractive. He's been doing it since we were teenagers."

I stare holes through Dougie, and he mimics Nolan, also throwing up his hands in my direction.

"Katie, like Nolan says, we've been searching for good help, and I'm just overjoyed to let you know we've found it."

Another smug grin, followed by an eye roll from me. There aren't any other customers at the bar so Dougie excuses himself to go restock.

"Sorry," Nolan whispers with a scrunched nose. "I was just trying to pay him a compliment. She really did give us great service. I didn't dare tell Sammie and her mother that our waitress used to work for Palmer. That would have been a nightmare."

"Oh, I'm just giving Doug a hard time. It's what we do. So, speaking of Sammie, how did it go?" I ask, anxious to hear about if she dropped any bombshells.

"Well, she didn't show. I think she got cold feet."

The look in his eyes breaks my heart in two. He was so excited about this interview.

"Nolan, I'm so sorry. What did she say? Did she contact you at all?"

"No, she didn't, and I think her mom was worried she'd back out because she texted me first thing this morning to see if I'd heard from Sammie. I thought it was odd, especially because it was so early, but I assumed she just went for a walk to clear her head or something. I didn't hear from either of them again, and now they aren't returning my texts."

The door chimes, and an old regular I haven't seen since moving back to Grady walks in. His name is Don Stanley, and he's lived here his entire life. He used to come in with his wife, Sally, until she passed away of cancer a few years back and he started staying home.

"Well if it isn't Don Stanley!" I say, clapping my hands together. "I haven't seen your handsome face in years!"

"Katie Bug Benard! I know you're just sweet on me

because you heard I started getting my railroad pension," he says, waddling over to give me a hug as I come out to greet him. "Tell me you're not old enough to be behind this bar."

"You don't even want to know how old I am, Mr. Stanley. Have a seat and meet my friend, Nolan. Do you still drink rum and Coke?"

Don shakes Nolan's hand and takes a seat on the barstool next to him.

"Better make it a Diet Coke. Doc Randall has been on my ass about the sugar," he tells me, and I smile. I'm sure Doc Randall would have a few things to say about rum consumption at lunch on a Friday as well, but it's not my job to butt in.

"So what brings you in today, stranger?" I ask, sliding his drink across the bar, followed by a Benard's Lakeside Inn coaster.

"I was listening to the police scanner, and it sounds like ol' Curtis Rivers found something interesting out on the lake. He just called it in. I wasn't doing anything productive, so I figured I'd come here and have a front row seat."

"A front row seat?" Nolan asks. "What do you think he found?"

"Well, Curtis tells some tall tales but they're usually about the size of the fish he claims to catch. I've got no reason to doubt him otherwise, and according to the call he made to the sheriff's office twenty minutes ago, Curtis Rivers found himself a dead body."

Thirty

I'M REMINDED that half the officers in the county are currently suspended, including Sheriff Nelson, when three Michigan State Police SUVs pull through the Benard's lot and down to the docks. Nelson has been the first to respond to any sort of commotion in this county for the last thirty years, and I'm sure it's killing him to not take part in it. I have yet to hear the details surrounding Lincoln Palmer's attack, but I can't imagine Nelson having anything to do with it. As long as I've known him, he's done what's right. I'm sure he despises Lincoln Palmer as much as the rest of us, but orchestrating an attack on him in his own jail doesn't sound like the Sheriff Nelson I know.

"What's all the commotion about?"

I spin from my spot by the restaurant window to see Dad.

"Dad, when did you get here?"

"Just came in through the back, sweetie. I forgot my damn phone charger at the lodge, so I figured I'd take a ride to come get it."

"You drove all the way from Marquette for a phone charger? Or did you want to check on your darling daughters and aren't admitting it because you're afraid we'll accuse you of being clingy?"

"You might be onto something, sweetie," he says, wrapping an arm around my shoulder. When he steps back, he notices Nolan standing at the end of the bar. "Nolan, my man! I downloaded that application you told me about, and it really does tell me where the coppers are hiding. I may never get pulled over again!"

"Or just spit balling here, you could drive the speed limit and then you wouldn't have to worry about speed traps," I say, shooting Nolan a look for telling my dad about the existence of such an app.

"So what are all the state boys doing here?" he asks, returning the attention to the view outside Benard's.

"According to old Don Stanley, they just got a call about a dead body found by Curtis Rivers."

"No shit . . . " Dad says with a low whistle. "This place is becoming the new south side of Chicago. No offense, Nolan."

"None taken, sir," Nolan replies, giving me a quick head shake once Dad turns back around.

"Nelson and the other guys are still suspended, so MSP is handling it, apparently," I say.

Within seconds, Curtis Rivers' boat comes into view. He's driving full throttle and has little Brogan wrapped up in a blanket, bundled safely under one of his arms. *Shit. I completely forgot Brogan was with him.* When they get closer to Benard's, he slows and ties his boat to the end of the dock, where the officers are waiting for him. He exchanges a few words with them before pointing back at the restaurant, seemingly straight at me, standing in the window. The officers nod, and Curtis picks Brogan up, still wrapped in his thick wool blanket and begins running toward the restaurant. I grab the first coat I can find on the hooks inside the kitchen door and throw it on, running out the door to meet him. I'm aware that half a dozen people are still in the restaurant, watching our every move through the window. Brenda is at my heels; I didn't even realize she'd arrived for her shift yet. We've all been too glued to the action outside.

"Curtis," I greet him, not knowing what else to say with Brogan in earshot.

"Buddy, what would you think about going inside with Miss Brenda and coloring me a new picture for the fridge? I bet if you behave, she'd even give you some hot chocolate," Curtis says, setting Brogan back down and bending to his level.

The small boy looks up at Brenda, and she plasters on the sweetest, most maternal face she can muster. "Now that sounds like some fun, Brogan!"

Thankfully, he goes along with it and reaches his hand out, knowing he must hold hers if he's going to walk through the parking lot. As they leave, I hear him asking her if he can have both marshmallows and whipped cream on top of his hot chocolate, and she says only if they don't tell his dad.

"I've got to go back out with the state boys. They are bringing in their own boats shortly. I marked the spot with my fish finder so we can find it easily. I don't think he saw anything, Katie, I don't. As soon as I realized what I was looking at, I turned the boat and told him I saw fish jumping on the other side. I pray he didn't see a thing. I don't know what I'm going to do if he did. My wife is going to kill me."

"Hey, hey. It's going to be okay. You did the right thing," I tell him, rubbing his arm awkwardly over his Carhart jacket. "How sure are you that it's really a body?"

"Katie, it wasn't just a body. It was that Spencer girl; I'm certain of it."

<h1 style="text-align:center">Thirty-One</h1>

"I CAN'T BELIEVE I just waited on her last night," says a tearful Chelsey with Dipshit Dougie hanging on her every word. There is no way this girl can be selfish enough to make Sammie's death about herself.

I glance up at one of the TVs above the bar, and the headline on TV6 reads Second Body In Two Months Found In Small Inland Lake, as if the two deaths are related. Benson's killer died in jail last week, and Sammie's still walks among us.

"They say tragedies happen in threes," Brenda says, barely above a whisper.

"Mom, what does that even mean? And I'd say we've had a few more than three tragedies in this town lately," Dougie tells his mother.

She simply shrugs and returns to wiping down a table by the window for the fourth time. If she scrubs it any harder, she's going to take a layer off the surface.

Curtis came to get Brogan after leading authorities to Sammie's body. A positive identification has yet to be announced, but Curtis swears on everything holy that he's certain it's Sammie. I didn't get much of a chance to chat with him because he understandably wanted to get Brogan home and figure out how much, if anything, he saw while they were out there fishing.

"Hey, I just heard," says Nicole, coming up behind me in the bar. "What in the actual fuck is going on in this town?"

I look around for eavesdroppers and then usher Nicole to the corner of the dining room so we can have some privacy.

"Nolan said Sammie was about to drop some bombs in her interview and then she didn't show up. That can't be a coincidence, right?" I ask her in a hushed tone.

"So somebody killed her to shut her up? That's some mafia shit," Nicole whispers back.

"Some mafia shit in Grady Lake. Who would have thought?"

"I was cleaning out Mae's apartment this morning and I found this. Thought you might want to put it in your room," Nicole says, handing me a picture I drew for her grandmother in the second grade. I was always honored that she thought highly enough of my drawing of the three of us together to frame it, but now I understand it was most likely for pure entertainment. If it weren't for the misspelled names labeling each stick figure, there's no way anyone could tell it was even supposed to be us.

"Nicole, this painting meant so much to you. I think you need to hang it up in *your* room. I insist."

"You did really capture the hints of hazel in my eyes here," she says, pointing to the two uneven black dots on the page. "I'm surprised you didn't get into art school."

"Get fucked. But also, are you okay after cleaning out her apartment? I know that couldn't have been easy. I wish you would have asked me to help."

She's kicking her Converse sneakers against the edge of the table next to her, avoiding eye contact with me. "I know you would have helped, KB. But I needed to do this on my own. I'm always depending on you or Mae or Dad for everything, and this month has taught me that I really need to learn how to do things myself."

"Well, that breaks my heart but also makes me feel like my little Nicole is growing up," I say, trying to get a smile out of her.

"Fuck you," she responds with a slight grin. "Where's khaki pants?"

"He and Karli went to the station to give statements. They had dinner with Sammie and her mom last night, and they want to help however they can."

"Do you think they are the killers and they're just trying to help so they aren't suspects?"

"Yes, Nicole, that's exactly what I think is going on. You should have been a detective."

"People tell me that all the time," she responds, tipping her baseball hat in my direction before walking back to the kitchen, kicking an unsuspecting Dougie in the back of the knees on her way.

I'm finally clocking out for the day, although I'll ask Lou to take the last hour or so off my timecard because I performed zero actual restaurant duties. We've all been too preoccupied by the drama unfolding outside. The morning sun and above freezing temperatures have melted a majority of the snow we received yesterday and created a muddy mess of our parking lot. The countless police and news outlet vehicles have only made it worse. A bystander may think Lou is angrily pacing back and forth because of the discovery of a body on our lake, but I know it's because she's worked up over the dirt everyone is going to track in from outside.

Dad is still hanging around and has taken a seat at the end of the bar, but he's drinking coffee rather than scotch, which is a welcome sight. All of our eyes turn to the parking lot when we see Nelson's Grady Police cruiser pull in. He gets out of the vehicle in full uniform and walks over to the state police officers near the dock. They each shake his hand and appear to fill him in on the scene, pointing to the lake in the direction of the cove where Sammie's body was discovered. He nods, makes a few notes, and shakes their hands again. We all make ourselves look busy when we realize he's not walking back to his vehicle, but instead in the direction of the restaurant.

"Sheriff Nelson," I greet him when he walks in the front door. "It's nice to see you back in action." I regret the words as soon as they are out of my mouth, as I'm not even sure I'm supposed to know he was suspended, but he barely seems to react.

"A prisoner died on my watch. They wouldn't be doing their jobs if they didn't take us out of the equation and complete an investigation. We get it."

"I'm just sorry you had to deal with that on top of everything else," I tell him.

"It forced me to take a few days off, which I haven't done all year. The wife was actually thankful for it, but a few days were enough and now she's ready to get me out of her hair," he replies with a grin. "It sounds like I'm going to have some long hours ahead of me with today's developments, and I sure could use a piece of Deb's strawberry rhubarb pie first."

"Sit anywhere you'd like," I tell him, gesturing vaguely to the dining room. "I'm just clocking out, but Dougie is training a new hire so take it easy on her."

Nelson's eyes search the room before landing on Chelsey, wiping down the bar in her new Benard's uniform.

"Chelsey Pritchard? That's your new hire?"

"You know Chelsey?" I ask, not even trying to hide the surprise on my face. To the best of my knowledge, Nelson never hung out at Palmer's Resort.

"It's a small lake," he replies, making a beeline for the bar.

She doesn't appear thrilled to see him, which makes me wonder what kind of trouble she's been in with the law. He says a few hushed words to her, and she listens intently before they are interrupted by Dougie, who takes Nelson's drink order and walks off. Even my dad seems to notice the awkward energy between the two while Doug goes in the kitchen to get Nelson's coffee and pie. When he returns and sets the mug and plate in front of Nelson, my dad strikes up a conversation with them both. They are most likely talking about Sammie, as they keep gesturing back toward the lake and shaking their heads. Chelsey is silent but hanging on their every word.

I decide to finally leave the restaurant, as I've had enough drama for one day. I check my phone before I shove it in my coat pocket to confirm there are no new messages from Nolan. I sure hope the investigators aren't keeping him and Karli at the station any longer than needed.

"I just saw the news," Malorie says as I walk in the lodge. It's still odd to see her sitting in front of the television. "Do they know who it is?"

"Curtis Rivers is the one who found the body. He says it's Sammie Spencer."

Mal gasps and clutches a hand over her heart. "Is he sure?" she asks.

"Says he is. It's so strange; Nolan had dinner with her last night and said she was ready to talk. She was going to give a full description of the second kidnapper on the podcast today."

"I saw her last night, through the window. She was standing in the field between the lodge and the restaurant, taking pictures of the snow," Malorie tells me, staring at the window next to the balcony door and replaying the scene in her head.

"What time was this?" I ask her.

"When you were gone with Nolan. It was after dark but not too late because I was in bed by ten."

"Did you see anyone else out there at all after dark?" I ask.

She thinks for a moment.

"I saw two of the cooks after their shifts, but they just went straight to their cars and left. Dougie and the new girl left at the same time and sat in Dougie's car for a while before she got out and went to her own. Oh, and Dad stopped by. He forgot his phone charger."

The same charger he told me he drove to Grady *today* for. Why would he lie about something as simple as a phone charger? I don't tell Malorie about it; the last thing she needs is something new to stress about.

Thirty-Two

BY SUPPER TIME, Nolan is seemingly still at the police station. I decide to drive down there because unless he's getting questioned by out-of-town investigators, chances are I went to high school with whoever is holding him there. A few threats and I'll have him released in no time.

Sure enough, I see his car outside as I pull into a spot near the door. When I enter the small brick building, I'm greeted by the same receptionist I've seen here for at least twenty years.

"Miss Bethany! What are you doing working so late?" I ask.

"I've switched to the midday shift so I can watch my soaps and still be home for dinner. Eleven to six and Melvin loves it. I haven't set an alarm in years."

"Well. That's the life, Miss Bethany. Hey, can you tell me who is questioning that podcaster from Chicago?" I don't use his real name because I know everyone in Grady is referring to him otherwise.

"Nelson's back there with him now. Want me to buzz in and see if they're almost done?"

"Nelson's back there questioning witnesses already? He was just at our place eating pie. He moves quick."

"Making up for lost time," Bethany says with a wink. She picks up the handheld phone on the desk in front of her, punches a few buttons, and tells Nelson I'm up front asking about Nolan. Shockingly, he tells Bethany to "just send me back," which is more than slightly unorthodox for a police interview.

When I walk back to the interrogation room, I knock once and Nelson shouts for me to come in. He's got his boots kicked up on the table and both Nolan and Karli are laughing hysterically at something he has just said. This doesn't feel like a police interview; it's more like old friends catching up over a round of beers. Or more accurately, lukewarm cans of pop from the ancient machine in the hallway. I try my best to match their jovial mood.

"I baked cupcakes with nail files inside so I could spring these two out, but it doesn't seem like I'm going to need them after all," I announce, taking a seat in the empty chair next to Nelson. "Did you decide to give these two a job here, or are they just refusing to come home?"

This gets another laugh from the room. To say I'm confused would be an understatement. They are supposed to be giving information about a young girl who just died, not having comedy hour at the Grady Jail.

"Well, we just found out there may not be a need for any interrogation. Early indications are that Sammie Spencer's death was an accident. She was seen by several witnesses taking pictures of the snowfall over the lake last night and we think she got too close and fell in," Nelson tells me.

"Curtis finds a body floating in the lake of a young girl who is about to possibly name her second kidnapper and we're calling it an accident?" I say before thinking twice.

"She wasn't floating, Katie. Bodies don't float in this

weather. Her foot, still laced up in her winter boot, was tangled in the bramble in Firekeeper's Cove. We think the fresh snow probably disguised the line between land and water and she stepped right in and fell face down. She tried to free herself, but her leg wouldn't budge," Nelson explains, sliding crime scene photos across the table to me which, thank goodness, do not show anything above the waist of her jeans. Sure enough, her leg is jammed into the tangled branches that lie a few feet below the surface of the cove. I've gotten into some real trouble when I've driven one of our boats too close to land in that very cove.

"And nobody heard her scream?" I try my luck with one more hole in the theory. This time Nolan jumps in.

"People don't actually scream when they are drowning. That just happens in the movies. They surprisingly stay pretty silent."

I look to Nelson for confirmation, and he nods. "And as far as this 'second kidnapper,' we have reason to believe there wasn't one. We aren't sure if she was disoriented from the drugs Palmer injected her with or just looking for a little attention. I don't want to think of the third theory, which is that she was involved with Palmer in a manner similar to your sister and was trying to protect him, but the evidence points to Lincoln acting alone."

Although the accusation stings, the only insane theory on that list is that she'd make up a second kidnapper for attention. C'mon.

"Your friend Nolan just brought up an excellent theory. You remember those electronic journal entries we found, detailing her love for Dougie? What if she was using Dougie as a code name for Palmer in case her parents somehow got into the app?"

"And Dougie would be the better option in this scenario?"

I can't help but get a quip in, even in this situation. I probably need to work on it.

"Well, he's a thirty-nine-year-old single man, as opposed to Palmer who was nearly three times her age with a wife and a family. I wouldn't be surprised if Nolan is onto something here."

"I guess I'm going to have to start referring to you as an investigative journalist, rather than 'that podcaster,' eh?" I ask, shooting him a professional smile across the table. "How is Mrs. Spencer taking it?"

"At first, as you'd expect. Crying, screaming, throwing accusations around. After Sammie's body was removed, we took Brandi Spencer to the scene and showed her the crime scene photos. She insisted on stepping in the water herself and nearly got tangled within seconds. She seemed to accept the theory after that and thanked us all for our assistance," Nelson answers. "I think part of her is relieved that daughter didn't die at the hands of someone else. I can't imagine the emotions that woman has gone through in the last two months."

It's unfathomable that this entire state was on a desperate search for Sammie, collectively rejoicing when she was found alive, only for her to die in a freak accident a month later. It reminds me of that documentary about the man in Oklahoma who served over a decade on death row for a murder he didn't commit. His supporters fought tooth and nail for his release, and after a lengthy process, he was a free man, only to die unexpectedly shortly after. The man barely got to enjoy his freedom.

"I heard The Moose Trap is doing free chicken and dumpling soup tonight," Nolan tells me.

"Well, aren't you becoming quite the local?" I respond as

lighthearted as possible, my stomach still in knots from the revelations about Sammie.

"I could use a stiff drink," Karli adds.

"You kids mind if an old timer joins you? I could use one, too."

"Of course," I respond, and the unlikely group of us pile in our cars to have a night cap on one of the strangest days I've ever had.

Thirty-Three

I'M a little annoyed when Nolan doesn't accept my offer to ride with me to The Moose Trap, instead driving Karli. Maybe he is just overprotective about letting someone else drive his vehicle. I spend the ten-minute journey overanalyzing everything Nelson just told me. Could it really be possible that Sammie was also having a summer fling with Lincoln Palmer? He was a good-looking man who was also filthy rich; I suppose I could understand the attraction if I didn't hate him so much. Maybe Fallon Palmer thought she was rescuing Sammie, but she was actually complicit? Or maybe Sammie's relationship with Palmer began as an illicit affair until he held her against her will. There are so many possibilities; my head is spinning. Also, what the hell is going on with my dad? Why was he at the lake last night and again this morning, giving my sister and me both the same story? I've also got a weird feeling Nicole has been avoiding me, which is the complete opposite of her normally clingy behavior. I chalked it up to her grieving, but she's even been avoiding eye contact with me back at the lodge. It also occurs to me that Deb took an entire morning off just to get her driver's license renewed, something she could have done online. It's like everyone has lost their minds.

When our three cars pull into the bar in unison, Nolan exits his car, waits a beat for Karli, and then goes directly inside without waiting to walk me in. Are you kidding me? Is it a full moon? I'm near tears as I get out of my SUV and zip my coat up to fight the cold wind on my walk inside.

I take a deep breath before opening the door. It's fine; maybe Nolan isn't the gentleman I believed him to be. Maybe he doesn't feel as strongly for me as I do for him, and I misread the signals. Wouldn't be the first time.

I pull the heavy door with both hands and am so shocked by the sight, my body doesn't move for a full five seconds. It's like my mind isn't comprehending the scene and I'm frozen in confusion.

It's everyone in this life who I love dearly, standing together, yelling "Surprise," with a bar full of balloons, cake, and gifts. I steal a glance at my watch and want to pass out when I realize the date. Tomorrow is my birthday. I have been so preoccupied with everything going on, I didn't even realize.

When another few seconds go by without me moving an inch, everyone moves toward me, drinks in their hands and smiles on their faces.

"Malorie? You're here?" I say when I see my sister.

"I know everyone here; it's okay," she says with a reassuring smile. She hugs me tightly, and that's when I snap out of it. It all makes sense. A surprise party.

My dad moves forward, placing his hands on my and my sister's backs. "You almost busted me with that phone charger story, didn't you Katie Bug? I was smoking my famous brisket over here and needed to check on it. When I saw all the commotion at the dock, it didn't occur to me that you'd be inside, and I'd have to come up with an excuse."

"Dad sent me a text that just said, 'saw Katie, told her I

forgot my phone charger,' and I thought he meant he saw you and Nolan the night before. I completely messed that up telling you he was also here the night before for the same reason," Mal explains, and I blow out the breath I have been holding all day. Somewhere, in the back of my worried mind, I'll admit that the thought of Dad mysteriously being seen right before Sammie's death bothered me. It feels so foolish now.

Nolan walks over and gives me the sweetest hug, kissing me on the temple as we part. "It killed me to avoid you today, but I'm the worst liar. I would have ruined the whole thing!" He laughs. Malorie and Dad excuse themselves to go sample the smoked brisket, which leaves Nolan and me alone at the entrance to the bar. Everyone else has gone back to their own conversations, giving me breathing room, which is nice. It all still feels like a dream. I can't believe they pulled this off without me suspecting a thing.

"We talked about calling it off with everything that went down this morning, but Lou said if she canceled family events every time there was a tragedy in town, you'd never celebrate anything again."

"She probably just didn't want to lose her deposit on renting the bar out," I tease.

"That, too," Nolan says, leaning forward to steal a quick kiss. "Oh, speaking of bad liars—"

"You little bitch! That was horrible. It was the hardest thing I've ever done," exclaims Nicole as she jumps between Nolan and me, a cold beer in her hand.

"That's why you've been so distant," I say, putting the pieces together. "I knew you were grieving, so I backed off, but damn. It just wasn't like you to be so cold."

"It was the only option, KB. One night alone with you and I would have sung like a bird. I had to avoid you. Khaki pants threatened my life."

"Oh, I did not. And quit calling me that," he says, before reddening slightly when he realizes he is, in fact, wearing khakis.

"These decorations are amazing," I muse, admiring the green and gold balloons and Green Bay Packers helmet cake. It is the same theme I've had for just about every birthday since I was nine.

"Deb picked them up in Marquette. I could have killed her when she told you she was getting her license renewed. I thought you'd see right through it but turns out you're just as dumb as I suspected," Nicole boasts. I roll my eyes and point to the bar. I think Nolan and I could both use a drink after this hell of a day.

Karli is already at the bar, drinking whiskey and talking with Dougie and Chelsey, who appear to have graduated their relationship from flirtation to public displays of affection. I guess she finally gave in to the magic charms of Dipshit Dougie. I wonder what her former roommate will think of the news. I slide in next to them so Nolan and I can place our orders when I hear Chelsey say, "Oh, thank God."

"Yeah, we were all relieved to hear that there wasn't a more nefarious explanation. It's tragic, but it sounds pretty cut and dry. It was an accident," Karli explains.

"It's just such a relief that we don't have to worry about another monster out there. I think we're all still scarred from finding out about Lincoln Palmer. I mean, I worked for the man for years and didn't suspect a thing," Chelsey says, taking a drink from her daquiri. Not sure who drinks daquiris in November, but whatever.

"You worked with that man for over a decade and really never suspected he was up to something?" I ask, the courage coming before I've even had any liquid.

Chelsey stares me directly in the eyes before answering. "Not once."

Dougie senses the tension in a rare moment of social awareness and changes the subject. "Did we really surprise you, or did you know?"

"Dougie, I didn't even remember that it was my birthday week. My head has been all over the place. It was definitely a surprise, and I can't thank you guys enough."

"Dad, Lou, and Nolan pretty much planned the whole thing. I just showed up and ate brisket," he says.

"Sounds about right," I answer. Nolan now has our drinks, two hot toddies, just like we had several nights ago, and I get a rush when his arm wraps around my waist after handing me the drink. I love the thought of him working with Lou and Dad to plan a surprise party for me. I'm not sure a man I've been involved with has ever done something so kind. I'm glad they pulled it off because we all needed a night to let off some steam.

Everyone seems to be having the time of their lives, except for Malorie, who keeps getting nearly strangled by hugs from the aunts who are so happy to see her in a public setting. She keeps asking them to stop but they keep hugging. Dad and Sheriff Nelson are talking in depth about his meat smoking process, Nicole is doing her best to ruin Chelsey's impression of Dougie, Karli has struck up a conversation with Jay, the bartender, and the remaining guests are employees of Benard's, who all seem to be enjoying themselves. They are even playing my favorite station, and I cheer when "Steal Away" by Robbie Dupree comes on. Nicole and I have drunkenly danced every time this song has played in our presence since high school. Tonight is no different as she takes the drink from my hand, sets it on the table next to hers, and spins me in a circle.

For the next few minutes, we steal the show doing our semi-choreographed dance moves that work for most easy listening hits, not just those sung by Robbie Dupree. Nolan attempts to join us, but a few moves in his shoulder begins hurting so he excuses himself and watches us in amusement from his spot at a pub table.

When the song is over, I make my way over to my dad and Sheriff Nelson, who are sitting at a table telling stories about how good smelting used to be around here in the nineties. I'd rather talk about paint drying, but they happen to have a full pitcher of beer and an extra glass, so I join them momentarily to pour myself one. When I reach over the candle in the middle of the table to grab the pitcher, Dad says, "Oh no, KB, you're going to light yourself on fire on your birthday," and I laugh so hard, I blow the candle out, which gets a chuckle from both men.

"I'm going to light it again, but you have to be more careful. I told the fire department they could have the night off," Nelson says with a wink. He reaches into the pocket of his Sheriff's uniform and pulls out a small silver lighter, his initials engraved on the side. He holds the candle at an angle and with one flick, it's reignited.

"Damn, Nelson. You still have yours, too? We need to get rid of these. It only makes me think of the piece of shit who gave them to us," Dad says.

"I can't believe we stood in that bastard's wedding. We've known him all our lives and didn't have a clue," Nelson responds.

I reach over from my seat and scoot the slim trash can from the end of the bar to our table, and both men nod and throw their lighters in the bin, which are hopefully the last traces of Rich Lowery that remain in their lives. It's time to move on.

Thirty-Four

"I WANT to talk to you girls about something," Lou tells Malorie and me in the corner of the bar. She rarely drinks, so the brandy slush has softened her edges tonight. Mal and I nod, curious as to what else she could have to tell us. "Malorie, a few weeks before you were found, we hired a new dock worker named Robbie. He was one of the best employees we'd ever had at Benard's; everyone adored him. Unfortunately, we found out he was moonlighting as a nineteen-year-old Pablo Escobar."

"I don't think Escobar sold pills, Lou. It was cocaine," I correct her.

"You know what the hell I mean. The kid was trying to make a few extra bucks for college and had no idea that the pills he was selling to men like Rich and Lincoln were being used for such evil. He thought they just liked to get high. I got a chance to talk to him last week. His lawyer has negotiated his charges down to a misdemeanor, and he wants to make amends with the family."

I look at Malorie, who is processing the information. "Mal, I'll follow your lead on this one. He really is a good kid, and I believe that he never would have sold them drugs had he known."

"Are you wanting to hire him back?" Mal asks Lou.

"Well, I wanted to talk to you girls about it first. I already ran the idea past Deb and Brenda, and you know how quick those two softies are to forgive. Anyway, they are on board with letting him come back as long as it's okay with the both of you."

Malorie and I look at each other and shrug our shoulders.

"If he's as good of an employee as you two say, I don't see why we can't give him a second chance. I hope the public curiosity dies down by spring so I can work at Benard's again. After so long without fresh air, I'd love dock duty. I can work with the kid and keep an eye on him."

"So it's settled. We are bringing Robbie back, and I never have to work dock duty again. Cheers," I say, clinking my glass with both of theirs and walking away, ignoring their protests.

When we heard Robbie was arrested for selling pills to Lincoln and Rich, I didn't want to believe it. He really is one of the hardest working employees we've ever had and, from what I've seen, comes from a great family. He didn't exactly fit the stereotype of being a drug dealer. I'm confident he learned his lesson and would be happy to welcome him back.

Everyone at this party knows me well enough to accept that I won't be opening gifts in front of a room of onlookers. That is my nightmare. Nolan helps me load them into the back of my Highlander shortly after I announce that my social battery is running low and I'm ready to go home.

"Hold on one second," he says as we load the last gift in. We pause as he closes the liftgate and leans on my car.

"What is this about?" I say when he doesn't move or speak for nearly a minute.

He looks at his watch and smiles.

"Okay, it's midnight. Happy birthday, Katie Benard. You are the most special woman I have met in my entire life."

I am shivering so much from the cold, my teeth are chattering. He unzips his coat and opens it so I can wrap my arms around him before he closes the coat around me. Once again, we share the most magical kiss in the parking lot of The Moose Trap as snow begins to fall.

"I went to Marquette to buy your birthday gift the other day and drove around to check the town out. It seemed like a pretty good transition spot if I decide to move out of the city. It has everything I'd need without having the headaches of Chicago . . ."

I gasp.

"Really? You'd consider it?" I recognize the desperation in my voice and change course. "I mean, I guess that would be fine." I can barely get the words out without smiling.

"I can do the podcast work from home, so really I can live wherever I'd like. Having a break from the rent I pay in the city would be nice, and I'd be closer to the woman I'm dangerously close to admitting I love."

I can't help but gasp again. For so long, I believed I was foolish for wanting this feeling. My ex, Dave, told me once that my problem was that I wanted everything to be like the movies. He said it was probably because I had a traumatic youth, so I was searching for magical relationships that only existed on screen.

Tonight, I know Dave was wrong because the joy I have in my heart for the man standing in front of me would put any rom-com to shame. He is everything I've been searching for and, as the saying goes, he came along when I was least expecting it. This birthday party is the start of my new life.

We now know that Lincoln Palmer most likely acted alone, both when he kidnapped and murdered young girls and also when he killed his own son.

Sammie Spencer's death was an accident.

We know the true story about how our mother died and, although tragic, she knew Malorie was still alive before she passed.

The man who held my sister captive for twenty years is behind bars, and if we can get through the trial, it should be the last bit of unresolved business looming over our little town. We can finally move forward and begin to heal.

I've only had one hot toddy and one beer, so I feel sober enough to drive the half mile to the lodge, but I worry about Dougie, so I peek my head into the bar while Nolan hops in my passenger seat and warms up my car. Everyone is collecting their belongings and tipping the bartender as I search the bar for my cousin, who was three sheets to the wind an hour ago when I last talked to him. I find him in the corner sucking face with Chelsey. *Fantastic.* I approach them as they are kissing and, without pulling away, Chelsey makes eye contact with me while she's kissing Dougie. She doesn't blink, simply stares me down. It is the strangest thing, and something about the look in her eyes sends chills down my spine. Reluctantly, I tap his shoulder and when he spins to face me, he is a complete mess. Bloodshot, glazed over eyes and slurred speech.

"Hey, dipshit, why don't you come home with Nolan and me, and we'll pick up your car in the morning?"

"Nah, KB, I'm fine."

I laugh, albeit condescendingly because he's trashed, and Chelsey stares daggers through me.

"He said he's fine," she says in a smug tone. "He's an adult; he can make his own decisions."

"Yeah, you *women* in my life have been bossing me around long enough. It's time I do what I want," he says, holding the table for balance. These are not words that would ever come from Dougie's mouth. She has fed him this bullshit. I can't believe it. *Who is this woman?*

"Doug, if you get pulled over, I'm not bailing you out. Why don't you give me your keys, and you can walk back if you don't want to ride with me?"

"I've got his keys; I'll drive him," Chelsey says, and although she sounds like a stone-cold bitch, she also seems stone-cold sober. I make eye contact with him for several seconds before turning to leave, and although he's hammered, I know he felt the seriousness of the situation because I hear him mumble to her that he's ready to go home as I'm walking away.

Thirty-Five

BANANA AND CHOCOLATE chip pancakes for breakfast have been a birthday tradition for the "children" in this family my entire life. We get up early, Lou cooks, and we let the non-family employees open the restaurant while we gather in the lodge and eat stacks of pancakes topped with locally made maple syrup and overflowing heaps of whipped cream.

This morning, Karli and Nolan are invited to my birthday breakfast, as well as Dad and Sheriff Nelson. I'm overjoyed when Lou announces that she's invited Robbie to join us after learning that he's had a falling out with his own family after his arrest. We are happy to invite him into ours and are strong believers in second chances. Brenda peeks in Dougie's room and speaks to him briefly before returning to us with disappointment on her face, announcing that he's "not feeling up to" celebrating with us (i.e., he's got a hangover from hell). He's never missed a birthday. I'm just glad Chelsey isn't here. She gave me such a weird feeling last night, and I plan to talk to the rest of the family about it once everything settles down.

Everyone is standing in line, filling their plates with

pancakes and mugs with coffee. Laughter and loud voices echo through the lodge, and I'm happy to think that it's making Dougie's headache worse. That's what he gets for missing my birthday breakfast. I'm grabbing orange juice from the fridge when there's a light tap at the door and Robbie steps in.

"Sorry, Lou told me to come on in," he says sheepishly.

"Don't be sorry, you little jerk, get your drug dealing ass in here," Nicole tells him, putting him in her signature headlock that's normally reserved for Dougie. Lou pulls her off Robbie with an eye roll and gives him a pat on the back.

"Good to have you back, kid."

"Good to be back, ma'am."

"You must be the famous Robbie," Malorie says, stepping forward to shake his hand.

"And you're literally famous," he says to her, wide-eyed. He's embarrassed as soon as the words leave his mouth, but we all get a kick out of it. To the teenagers of Grady Lake, the story of Malorie Rose Benard was a legend they told around the campfire and now he's standing in her kitchen. I can't imagine the gravity of it all to a stranger.

"Well, get used to me because we're working dock duty together this season, and spoiler alert —we won't be selling pills," she tells him with a playful smile. His face is flushed, and he begins issuing an apology before Nicole cuts him off.

"Robbie, let us make fun of you for a few weeks, and then we'll get over it."

"Fair enough," he says, his smile indicating the relief of being accepted back into our presence. "I can't wait to get back to work."

"Well, that makes one of us," Malorie says, handing him a plate and guiding him forward toward the pancakes.

We aren't a religious family, but we all bow our heads as Sheriff Nelson says a blessing that's actually quite lovely. He thanks God for reuniting Malorie with her loved ones, for our ability to forgive Robbie, and for welcoming Nicole into our family. Several tears are shed by the time we all mumble *Amen*.

I can't get over how well Nolan fits in with my family. The aunts adore him, Malorie treats him like he's already married in, and Nicole tolerates him, which is more than she's done for anyone else I've dated. We spend the morning telling stories, jokes, and reminiscing about mom. The irony is not lost on me that these breakfasts are usually spent recounting our favorite memories involving Malorie, and now she's here to join us.

Reluctantly, I agree to open my gifts from last night's party but only if everyone goes about their business and doesn't stare at me while I unwrap them. Nolan and Karli sit on the sectional couch with me while everyone else honors my wishes and disperses around the lodge to drink their coffee and converse, giving me space. Dad walks up to Nolan with an empty trash bag and tells him I'm his problem now. He's confused until he realizes Dad just wants him to keep up with the wrapping paper disposal.

The great thing about my family is that we are all great at giving practical gifts. We don't buy three-hundred-dollar handbags or jetted foot baths that will never get used. My birthday presents this year include a gas gift card, an Amazon gift card, jumbo-size shampoo and conditioner, and a new coffee mug with a snarky saying about hating mornings. Nicole, per usual, has found something around her house and wrapped it up for me. This year it's a dish that holds jewelry and I suspect it may have even come from Mae's apartment. Karli, whom I would never expect to give me a gift, bought me a bag of my favorite Door County Coffee.

The last present is from Nolan, and Karli does a horrible job of acting like something across the room needs her attention so she can give us privacy while I unwrap his gift. I slowly open the medium-sized box while he watches in anticipation.

There are several small items in the box, the first is a gift certificate to The Moose Trap. I laugh when I see it's just a handwritten piece of paper from Jay in the amount of twenty-five dollars and a horribly drawn picture of a moose.

"They don't sell gift certificates, do they?" I ask.

"They do now," he answers with a smile, and if it weren't for this room full of people, I'd kiss him.

The second item in the box is an oversized bottle of fish oil supplements. I throw my head back and laugh when I see that the pills are "smaller in size and with less fishy taste," because the size and taste are two reasons I've refused to take fish oil, despite Nolan's insistence that it could help with my dry eyes, among a dozen other health benefits.

"Okay, okay; I'll give them a try," I tell him, still smiling.

I pause when I unwrap the tissue and see the last item in the box. It's a makeshift radio comprised of two metal cans and a string connecting them. My name is written on one can and Malorie's on the other. I barely remember telling him the story, but I guess I must have. One of the last plans that Mal and I had before she disappeared—we had seen two characters in a movie use them and thought it would be so funny to whisper to each other from our beds across the room. We planned to steal two empty cans from the restaurant the following week and try them out. I told Nolan that after Malorie was gone, I'd stare at her empty bed, sick over the fact that we never saw our plan to fruition. It would have been one more happy memory I could have had of my sister, but we just never got around to making them. This is the most thoughtful gift he could have given me.

I wipe the tears from my eyes and give him a hug, my arms wrapped tightly around his shoulders. "I don't care that we are in our thirties; I'm making her use these with me," I tell him.

I excuse myself while he is fulfilling his duties of wrapping paper pickup and go find Mal. I pray she remembers the significance of these tin cans. I don't see her with the rest of the family, so I assume she's gone in our room for some peace and quiet. Since her return, she can only handle so much social interaction before needing a break. I crouch down and tiptoe toward our room with a plan to roll her can across the hardwood floor while holding my own. Assuming she remembers our plan twenty years ago, she's going to get the biggest kick out of this.

As I creep closer to our room, I hear two hushed voices and quickly realize it's Nicole and Malorie. It's odd to hear them talking alone in a room; they haven't had many interactions since Mal's return, and it's no doubt due to the delicate issue of Nicole being Rich's daughter. She's known and loved Mal her whole life and surely is having a hard time facing her after what her dad took from our entire family. Against my better judgement, I stop outside the door and listen to their conversation. I know I shouldn't snoop on something so private, but I can't help myself.

"You can't avoid me forever," Mal says to Nicole.

"I'm not avoiding you; I'm just trying to process some memories I have and sort everything out," Nicole responds.

"Sort everything out? You saw me, Nicole. You saw me in that basement and did nothing. I thought you were there to rescue me, and you turned back around and left me there to rot."

Epilogue

"HEY, Baker, I think I found something over here!" yells the young officer. The crime scene technicians have long since finished their search and documentation at the home of Richard Lowery, but Sheriff Nelson is convinced that his men can find more evidence and possibly the body of Malorie Benard's baby, who died during childbirth. It would take one ounce of goodwill for Lowery to admit where he buried the body, and they could all get out of the cold and go home to their families, but he's still refusing to talk.

"What have you got?" Baker asks, crouching down beside the officer.

He removes a large trunk, the kind everyone's grandparents use to have but nobody seems to buy anymore. With a few swipes, he knocks off the clumps of dark soil on top. The men look at each other in nervous anticipation. This could be it. Malorie Benard said Rich told her he buried the baby in an old shower curtain and this trunk would be the perfect size for a makeshift coffin. They both hold their breath as the young officer slowly opens the unlocked trunk with his gloved hand. They exhale when they see it's just a stockpile of old USB drives. Although relieved that it's not a shower curtain wrapped around tiny bones, they are intrigued by the discovery. What could be on these drives that would be important enough to bury underground?

They begin picking them up and reading the labels. Each has a date and a short description.

09/05/00 Nelson and Palmer at bunker 1

10/15/01 Palmer and female at bunker 2

01/05/02 Palmer and ??? removing body bunker 2

11/1/20 Palmer and female (employee?) bunker 1

"Holy shit. Do you think Nelson is . . . our Nelson?" asks Baker. "There's no way, right?"

The younger officer stares at the pile of drives. There must be at least two dozen. He's sick to think of what kind of footage is on them.

"Maybe just to be sure, we should call this into MSP instead of Nelson?"

The men continue to sort through the pile, reading each label before setting them aside. When they get to the bottom, there's an old folded up article from the *Mining Journal*, Marquette's daily newspaper. It's from 2004.

GRADY, MICHIGAN

THE NEWBORN WHO MADE HEADLINES AS THE UPPER PENINSULA'S FIRST BABY TO BE SURRENDERED UNDER THE STATE'S SAFE DELIVERY OF NEWBORNS LAW HAS BEEN ADOPTED.

THE LAW, WHICH WENT INTO EFFECT ON JANUARY 1ST, 2001, ALLOWS FOR A NEWBORN BABY TO BE SURRENDERED TO EMERGENCY FACILITIES WITHIN THE FIRST 72 HOURS AFTER BIRTH AND IS WIDELY CONSIDERED TO BE A SAFE ALTERNATIVE FOR DESPERATE PARENTS. THE SURRENDERING PARENT

CAN REMAIN ANONYMOUS AND ISN'T REQUIRED TO GIVE ANY ADDITIONAL INFORMATION WHEN LEAVING THE CHILD WITH EMERGENCY PERSONNEL.

SHARI AND ROBERT STEPHENS, WHO HAVE BEEN UNSUCCESSFUL IN THEIR ATTEMPTS TO START A FAMILY ON THEIR OWN, ARE OVERJOYED TO BE THE NEW PARENTS TO YOUNG ROBERT STEPHENS JR, WHOSE ADOPTION WILL BE OFFICIAL THIS MONTH.

"WE DON'T KNOW THE SITUATION HIS MOTHER WAS IN TO GIVE UP THIS PRECIOUS CHILD AT BIRTH, BUT WE ARE OVER THE MOON THAT WE ARE GETTING THE CHANCE TO BE PARENTS. WE PROMISE TO GIVE LITTLE ROBBIE THE BEST LIFE IMAGINABLE."

THE STEPHENS FAMILY RESIDES IN THE SMALL COMMUNITY OF GRADY, MICHIGAN, AND TELL THE MINING JOURNAL THAT THEY WILL RAISE THEIR SON ON THE LAKE AND LOOK FORWARD TO PARTICIPATING IN OUTDOOR ACTIVITIES ONCE HE'S OLD ENOUGH. THEY ALSO SAY THEY ARE CONTENT NOT KNOWING THE IDENTITY OF THE PARENTS OF LITTLE ROBBIE BUT WOULD BE OPEN TO COMMUNICATING WITH THEM IN THE FUTURE IF THEY EVER CHOOSE TO REVEAL THEIR IDENTITIES AND PLAY A ROLE IN HIS LIFE.

Afterword

THE 3RD AND FINAL BOOK OF THE GRADY LAKE MYSTERY SERIES WILL BE AVAILABLE SUMMER OF 2024

Brandy Old Fashioned

- 3 dashes Angostura bitters
- 2 orange slices
- 2 brandied or marishino cherries
- 1 sugar cube
- 2 ounces brandy
- 7UP, Sprite, or club soda, chilled, to top

Muddle bitters, orange slices, cherries, and sugar cube in an Old Fashioned glass to combine.

Add ice to fill the glass, then add the brandy.

Top with the soda and stir to chill.

Garnish with a skewered cherry and an orange slice. Enjoy!

Moose Trap Hot Toddy

- ¾ cup water
- 2 ounces whiskey
- 2 tsp honey, to taste

- 2 tsp lemon juice, to taste
- 1 lemon round
- 1 cinnamon stick

In a teapot or saucepan, bring water to a simmer and pour into a mug.

Add the whiskey, honey, and lemon juice.

Stir until the honey has disappeared into the hot water.

Garnish with lemon round and cinnamon stick. Enjoy!

Benard's Brandy Slush

- 8 cups water
- 2 cups sugar
- 5 black tea bags
- 1 12-oz container orange juice concentrate, thawed
- 1 12-oz container lemonade concentrate, thawed
- 3-4 cups of brandy
- Sprite or 7UP

In a large pot, bring water and sugar to a boil, whisking to dissolve sugar.

Remove from heat and add tea bags.

Steep according to package instructions, three or four minutes, before discarding bags.

Let cool slightly before pouring into ice cream pail.

Stir in both concentrates and brandy. Mix to combine.

Cover pail with lid and freeze for 12 hours, or overnight.

When ready to serve, fill a glass halfway with slush and top with lemon lime soda. Enjoy!

Acknowledgments

Although I could ramble on for pages about how thankful I am to have so many loving, supportive, helpful people in my life, I recognize that readers only have so much patience, so I'll keep it short and sweet.

Hiring an editor is the best investment I've made in this career, and now I have two! Carly and Erika, thank you for helping me sleep at night. Thank you to my dear friend Brandon for creating the best covers that make me gasp each time I get the first peek. To my early readers, thank you for being my trusted group of feedback providers. I know it isn't easy.

I am sincerely grateful to my family and friends who have supported me since I, who had no business thinking she could write a book, announced that I wrote a book. You not once let me think that I couldn't do it. All authors should have the kinds of people I am lucky enough to surround myself with.

Cash, I'm so sorry that I walk out of the room several times when you give me feedback on my manuscript. Cheers to growing a thicker skin with each book; surely by my twelfth novel I'll be able to stomach the news, eh? Thank you for being the most honest, fun, intriguing man and also for coming with me to heaven, aka The Upper Peninsula.

Finally, to my readers: whether you found my books on social media, in a library or bookstore, or by word of mouth, I am so incredibly grateful you did. Time is a precious thing and I'm so honored you chose to spend yours by reading one of my books.

Speaking of precious time; I know leaving reviews can be tedious but, boy, do they help! Even if you have ten seconds to click a star rating wherever you review books, it would mean the world to me and helps me keep the lights on.

Thank you, reader, and I'll be back early in the summer with the final chapter of the Grady Lake saga.